AUDREY J.
COLE

THE
PILOT'S
DAUGHTER

ISBN: 9798741091494

RAINIER
PUBLISHING

CHAPTER ONE

Asha took a large bite of her rice when her phone chimed atop the table. She set down her fork and lifted her phone. A video message from a number she didn't recognize had popped up on her screen.

SeaTac's employee cafeteria was especially busy this time of day. In the seat next to her, one of her coworkers burst out laughing at a Tik Tok video she'd replayed for the third time. Asha reached into her pocket and placed a wireless earbud into her ear before opening the message.

The video began to play. A man filled the screen, shouting his allegiance to Al-Shabaab, the Islamist militant group that terrorized many parts of her native country. A black cloth covered the lower half of his face. He waved an assault rifle up and down as he yelled in Somali.

The video panned away from the man, and Asha recognized the rural village she'd lived in for the first twenty years of her life. Asha's breath caught in her throat as the video focused on several villagers on their knees in front of a wood hut, crying and begging for their lives. Another Al-Shabaab member, wearing a similar face covering, stood in front of the villagers with a rifle aimed at the man in the middle.

Laughter erupted again from Asha's cafeteria table. The video zoomed in on the villagers. They were her family. Her mother. Her father. Brother. Aunt. Uncle. Cousins.

The Al-Shabaab member who'd been shouting at the beginning of the video moved in front of the camera. His eyes stared into Asha's through the small screen of her phone. He spoke directly into the camera, only inches from his face.

"Asha."

She nearly dropped her phone when he said her name.

He backed away from the camera and held up a paper with a Seattle address. "You will go to this address tonight and pick up a package. Tomorrow, you will put the contents of that package in the AED on board Pacific Air Flight 385."

The video turned back to her relatives begging for their lives. The blast from the rifle made Asha jump in her seat. Blood splattered across the side of the Acacia hut and her uncle fell facedown into the dirt. Her aunt screamed hysterically as she stared at her husband lying in a pool of his own blood. The terrorist pressed his rifle into her chest and screamed at her in Somali to shut up.

The video swung back to the man holding the address. "Do this, and no one else in your family has to die."

"Boss, you ready?"

The video ended. Asha's mouth hung open in shock.

"Boss?"

She felt a hand on her shoulder.

"You okay?"

Asha was the only one still seated at their table. She looked up at her young coworker, Rosalyn, whose biggest concern was getting back to work. Asha tucked her phone into the side pocket of her airline cleaner uniform and stood from her chair.

"Yeah, fine. Let's go."

CHAPTER TWO

Asha got out of her car at the address the terrorists had given her. She closed her fingers tightly around the shoulder strap of her purse as she crossed the empty parking lot. The small, South Park warehouse looked as if it had been long abandoned. It was in an even more rundown part of town than where she lived. She had no idea what was waiting for her, and she didn't like being here alone.

She'd lied to her husband, telling him she had to stay late at work and asked if he could cook dinner for the girls and put them to bed. Hopefully, he wouldn't notice the missing overtime from her next paycheck. With traffic, it had taken her over an hour to find the address. She stopped at the metal door in front of the building.

Maybe she should just go home. Or go to the police. What if someone was waiting to kill her? But that video of her uncle's murder was real. And she understood that Al-Shabaab needed her to carry out a bigger plan. With a trembling hand, she knocked forcefully on the door.

She looked around when no one answered. She was alone. She tried the rusted door handle. The door rattled as she shook it, but the lock didn't budge. She looked back toward her car. The terrorists hadn't specified a time, just that she pick up a package at this address.

The late-August sky was beginning to darken as she walked around the side of the building. Not finding any doors, she rounded the rear of the warehouse. The hum of the few cars passing by grew softer. She came to a single door in the middle of the building. This time, she tried the door handle without knocking. It turned easily in her grip.

The door swung open. She stepped inside the large dark space onto a concrete floor. A musty smell filled her nose.

"Hello?"

There was no answer. Her heart pounded in her chest. Using her phone as a flashlight, she found a light switch on the wall. She turned it on, but nothing happened.

She looked around the large room and tried to focus on what she was supposed to find. A folding chair sat in one of the corners. A brown paper sack was perched on the seat.

Asha took careful steps toward the chair, worried about what was inside the bag. She wondered if it could be a bomb, waiting to explode after she picked it up. When she reached the chair, she assured herself that the terrorists weren't out to kill her. At least not yet. They needed her.

There was a sharp metal clang behind her as Asha started to open the bag. She spun around, shining her phone in front of her. There was no one there. She shined the light onto the floor and caught the movement of a small rat as it skittered across the dirty concrete.

Asha exhaled and turned back to the paper sack. She opened it and shined her light inside. Although she'd never held one in her hands, Asha recognized the black form of a pistol immediately. She felt herself relax slightly as she picked up the bag, glad it wasn't an explosive. She placed one hand underneath to support the gun's weight and hurried out of the warehouse.

Asha pulled back the comforter and slipped into bed next to her husband's sleeping form. She'd been glad to find him in bed. She didn't want to face him with more lies.

"How was work?" Aaden asked, as she turned onto her side.

"I thought you were asleep. Sorry if I woke you."

"That's okay." He yawned. "The girls will be glad to see you in the morning."

Asha felt sick to her stomach. "Me too. Good night."

"Good night."

A tear slid down her cheek as she faced away from him. His breathing changed to a rhythmic snore as Asha lay awake. An image of her uncle's final moments filled her mind when she closed her eyes. And the look of horror on her aunt's face after they executed him.

She wondered if she'd ever see her family again. Her thoughts drifted to the gun still in the brown bag that she'd tucked away in her glove compartment. For the sake of her relatives in Somalia, she forced herself not to think of the passengers who would be on Pacific Air Flight 385.

CHAPTER THREE

Cora stared out the rain-streaked windshield as her mother pulled into the *Departures* lane at SeaTac Airport. This was almost the very spot where she had seen her husband for the last time. "Are you sure you guys will be okay for a week? Maybe this wasn't such a good idea."

Her mother placed a reassuring hand on Cora's thigh. "Honey, we'll be fine. This will be good for you. And I've raised a few children of my own, remember?"

Cora unbuckled her seatbelt. "It's the first time I've left them since Wesley..." She couldn't bring herself to say it.

"I know. But it's important for you to go. And we're going to have a great time. Aren't we kids?"

Cora turned around to look at her son and daughter buckled into their car seats in the back of her mother's Range Rover.

"Yes!" Logan said.

Zoe was too engrossed looking out her window to respond.

Cora's mother smiled. "See? They'll be too busy having fun with Grandma to even notice you're gone. You better go so you don't miss your flight. It takes forever to get through security these days."

Cora nodded and climbed out of the car. She pulled her suitcase out of the trunk before she opened the rear door and kissed her kids good-bye.

"I love you guys. You be good for grandma, okay?"

Logan nodded.

"We will," Zoe promised.

Cora stepped onto the curb after closing the door. Her mom rolled down the passenger side window.

"Have a great trip, Cora. Try to enjoy yourself!"

Cora forced a smile and waved as her mother pulled away from the curb. She blinked back her tears and pulled her suitcase behind her as she went inside to check in for her Pacific Air flight.

Cora scanned the shelves at the airport newsstand, looking for something to get her mind off her worries. She settled on a new crime thriller set in Seattle. She grabbed a bag of corn nuts and smiled, thinking of how Wesley would always get them when they traveled. After purchasing them, she slipped the book and her snack into the side pocket of her carry-on. She slung the bag over her shoulder and started making her way to her gate.

She'd taken only a few steps when she felt a hand on her shoulder.

"Excuse me."

Cora turned to see an attractive man in a suit. He stood a few inches taller than her.

"I think you dropped this," he said.

She lowered her gaze to his outstretched hand, recognizing her newly-purchased novel.

"Oh. Thank you." She took the book and slid it into her bag.

"No problem." He offered her a pleasant smile before she turned and continued walking to her terminal.

Cora found an empty seat when she reached her gate and spent the next hour trying to lose herself in her novel. But she kept catching herself unable to concentrate, rereading the same paragraph about a young woman escaping from a castle several times. Finally, she gave up and placed the book on top of her carry-on. Her plane should be boarding any minute. She hadn't flown or left their children since Wesley's helicopter crashed last year, and this felt like a huge mistake. She wasn't ready.

Her phone pinged inside her purse. She pulled it out, seeing she had a message from her mom. *Having fun already.* She opened the message to see a photo of her kids holding up ice cream cones on her back porch. Cora smiled, despite the sinking feeling in her chest.

She would never have agreed to go if it wasn't so important. Wesley was most known for his multi-million-dollar cybersecurity company that he founded a decade ago, but his true passion was his humanitarian work. After American Samoa suffered a devastating cyclone early last year, he'd put nearly all his energy into relief efforts. He'd raised money, donated their own, flown over with supplies, and worked on the ground to help rebuild the community.

He'd been helping to rebuild a school when his helicopter crashed into the side of a mountain in bad weather.

"Passengers of Pacific Air Flight 385 with service to Honolulu, we are expecting an on-time departure," a female voice came over the PA system, interrupting Cora's thoughts. "And we will begin boarding in approximately forty-five minutes."

Cora's leg shook with anticipation of getting on the plane. With an airline pilot for a father, she'd never been afraid of flying. She'd flown countless times for as long as she could remember. Even taken flying lessons in college. But it felt wrong to leave her children. She was all they had left.

She'd never been to Samoa. Logan had only been eighteen months when the cyclone hit, and she had stayed home with the kids while Wesley traveled on his relief trips. She wasn't sure she was ready to see the place that had taken his life. But she needed to honor his life's work. He deserved that.

She crossed her legs and tried to force herself to relax. There was nothing dangerous about going on a commercial flight. It wasn't like getting in a helicopter in bad weather. Her dad would always say it was safer than driving a car.

CHAPTER FOUR

Asha stared at her glove box in the employee parking lot adjacent to the airport. She hadn't touched the pistol since she'd stowed it away last night. She reached into the compartment and retrieved the paper bag. She set it on the passenger seat before she pulled out her phone. There were no more messages from the terrorists.

She couldn't risk contacting her family in their remote village in Southern Somalia. A few of them had phones but calling them might jeopardize their safety. It was possible that Al-Shabaab had killed them already. But she had no doubt they would all be dead if she didn't do as they said.

What would happen to all those people on the plane?

Still holding her phone, Asha checked the status of Flight 385. It was on time and the gate number hadn't changed.

She hesitated before opening the video the terrorists had sent yesterday and pressed play. She closed her eyes at the end, knowing what was about to happen. Her aunt's screams coming through the phone were drowned out by the drone of a plane taking off overhead.

Asha made sure no one was around before she pulled the pistol out of the paper sack. She'd never held a gun before. Although heavy, it was smaller than most guns she'd seen on TV. Before she could change her mind, she zipped the small firearm into the front pocket of her neon green safety vest.

Asha stepped off the bus at the stop for the employee tunnel that led to the tarmac. She scanned her ID badge and pushed open the large metal door. She tried to look calm as she walked down the tunnel, knowing there was a chance she could be randomly checked. If she was searched and they found the gun on her, she'd be going to prison. And her children could grow up without a mother.

She checked the time on her phone. There wasn't much time. Flight 385 was scheduled to board in just under an hour.

An airport security officer stood at the far end of the tunnel. Asha kept her eyes straight ahead, praying he wouldn't stop her. She tried to think of a way to get out of it in the event he called her over.

Just keep calm. Asha forced herself to breathe as she neared the security officer. Would he notice the bulge in her front pocket? Was it obvious? She didn't dare look down to check. She wished she would've looked in a mirror after tucking the weapon into her vest.

"Excuse me," the security guard called out as she passed him.

Asha stopped. Maybe she should keep walking and pretend she didn't hear. *But then what? Run?* How far would she get?

"Sir, let me check your bag please."

Sir? Asha turned. The security guard was motioning to a man behind her.

She watched the man take his bag off his shoulder and walk toward the security guard. The guard looked in her direction. She gave him a weak smile and continued toward her locker room before he wondered why she was staring.

After depositing her purse in her locker, she went into the office across the hall and printed off the cleaning schedule for her shift, noting the gate number for Flight 385 hadn't changed.

She was five minutes late when she stepped onto the busy tarmac and found her cleaning crew waiting for her in the van that would transport them between gates.

"Hey boss," Rosalyn said from the back when Asha opened the passenger door.

"Hey." Asha climbed inside, acutely aware of the gun pressed against her abdomen. She turned to the driver as she pulled out her headset and turned it on. "Hi Todd."

A voice immediately crackled through her headphones. "Cleaning crew C, can you hear me?"

Asha pressed the talk button on her hand-held radio. "This is cleaning crew C. I hear you."

"Start at Gate A5. They've just disembarked."

"Got it," Asha said.

"Where to?" Todd asked.

Flight 385 was at A12. If they cleaned the plane at A5 first, there wouldn't be enough time to clean Flight 385 before it boarded. Another cleaning crew would be assigned. They had to get there first.

"We're starting at A12," Asha replied.

Asha finished cleaning the last window in the first-class cabin. She'd been careful not to knock the gun against anything for fear that it would go off in her vest pocket. Turning her back to the wall, she checked to make sure no one was watching.

Rosalyn was still cleaning in business class. She bent down to wipe down the seats, looking away from Asha. Asha had to move fast. She hurried toward the compartment containing emergency medical equipment.

Asha lifted the overhead compartment door just as another cleaning crew boarded the flight. She turned, trying not to look as startled as she felt.

"We were told to clean this flight," the lead said to Asha.

The supervisor's headset, identical to Asha's, hung around his neck.

Asha swallowed. "You must have the wrong gate number. We're almost done," Asha said as Rosalyn entered the first-class cabin.

"We're all done in the back," Rosalyn said.

"I don't have the wrong gate," the supervisor said.

Asha shrugged her shoulders. "Well, there must be some sort of mix-up." She was running out of time to plant the gun on the flight. She needed everyone off the plane. "Anyway, we're almost done." Asha forced a pleasant tone and hoped he didn't notice her voice was shaking. "Guess we did you guys a favor."

"Or you screwed up and there's another plane that didn't get cleaned. You better find out which one it was." He eyed Asha with a look of annoyance before turning out of the cabin, his crew following without a word.

"What's his problem?" Rosalyn asked.

"He said they were told to clean this flight. I'm sure they told me A12, but I'll double check with the head supervisor in a minute. Let's go."

Asha did a quick head count when they were back in the van to make sure her full crew was off the plane.

"What gate?" Todd asked.

The head supervisor's voice came through Asha's headset. "Cleaning crew C, A5 is still waiting for a turn-around clean. Where are you?"

Asha cleared her throat. "A5? I thought you said to start with A12."

"Nooo, I said A *five*. I need your crew there *now*. You've delayed their flight!"

"I'm so sorry. We're headed there now."

The supervisor's exasperated sigh came through Asha's headset. "You better move quick."

Asha turned to Todd, who was still waiting for her response. "They need us at A5, asap. Apparently, we were supposed to do that one first."

Asha looked down at her hands as Todd threw the van into reverse. "Oh, no. I forgot my disinfectant on that plane." She opened the passenger door as the van rolled back, causing him to stomp on the brakes.

"You could at least wait until I've stopped!" he exclaimed.

"Sorry," Asha said. "You guys head to A5, I'll meet you there."

Todd shook his head in disapproval as Asha climbed out.

"Fine," he said. "But next time, don't try to jump out while the van is moving."

"Sure. Sorry," she repeated. She closed her side door and speed-walked away from the van. She could only hope the flight crew hadn't boarded yet.

Asha flew up the stairs to the Jetway, an image of her uncle's final moments flashing in her mind. She felt the gun against the top of her thigh as she climbed the steps. She placed her hand gently against her front pocket to steady it.

When she got to the Jetway, she checked to make sure she was alone. The narrow passageway was empty, but Asha watched a flight attendant move toward the Jetway's entrance at the connecting gate. The woman slowed to make pleasantries with the gate agent standing to the side of the Jetway, and Asha hurried onto the jet.

None of the crew had boarded.

She went straight to the overhead compartment at the front of the first-class cabin. She pulled it open and sifted through the emergency medical equipment until she found the lime green AED. She checked behind her before she pulled the gun out from her vest. She could hear the flight attendant's roller bag coming down the Jetway.

Asha tore off the lid and stared at the small screen. There was no room to hide the gun. Where was she supposed to put it? The sound of the roller bag was getting

22

closer. She contemplated leaving it among the medical equipment, but what if the crew found it before takeoff?

She thought about those Al-Shabaab militants slaughtering her entire family if she failed. The roller bag had almost reached the aircraft. Asha placed the lid back onto the AED and was about to set the gun down loose in the compartment when a male voice called out from inside the Jetway.

"Mila! I didn't know you were on this flight."

The roller bag stopped. "Hey, Matt!" a female voice said from right outside the plane's entrance. "I traded last minute. How was your vacation?"

Asha moved a little to the side, making sure she couldn't be seen. She turned the AED over and pulled off the rear panel. This side was about an inch deep and filled with batteries. Asha swiftly pulled the batteries out, one by one, and dropped them into her pockets.

The man's voice grew closer as he told his coworker how amazing his trip to Cancun was. Asha slid the last battery into her pocket and shoved the gun into the small space, breaking a couple small pieces of plastic as she forced the lid down.

"What are you doing?"

Asha turned to see the female flight attendant, standing only a foot away from her as Asha closed the compartment. Asha lifted her cloth and cleaning solution from a leather seat.

"I left my cleaning supplies in here."

The woman eyed her with suspicion as Asha moved past her and her male counterpart standing behind her.

Asha smiled. "Have a nice day."

She tried to calm her breathing as she trod down the steps to the tarmac. She glanced back at the plane when she reached the bottom, knowing she'd never forgive herself for what would happen on that flight.

But it was done. She only hoped she'd saved her family.

CHAPTER FIVE

Cora had barely gotten to the second chapter of her new novel when the announcement came over the Intercom.

"Passengers for Pacific Air Flight 385, we would like to invite all those seated in first class to board at this time. We will begin our general boarding shortly."

Cora stood from her seat. She slung her carry-on bag over her shoulder as she moved slowly toward the Jetway. She thought about turning around and going home to her children. But she'd be letting Wesley down. He deserved to be honored. Remembered.

She held up her phone and scanned her electronic ticket when she reached the gate agent.

"Thank you. Have a nice flight," the woman said.

Cora walked down the Jetway, trying to ignore the anxious feeling in her stomach. *I'm doing this for Wesley,* she told herself. *And I'll be home with the children in less than a week.*

She was greeted by a platinum blonde flight attendant when she reached the plane.

"Good afternoon," the woman said.

Cora forced a smile before finding her seat. *Everything's going to be fine.*

Cora settled into her window seat and pulled out her book. On her way to her seat, she'd recognized the woman sitting across the aisle from her. Cora thought she'd recognized her at the gate, but now she was sure. She was Alana Garcia, billionaire Eddie Clarke's girlfriend. The young woman wore little makeup and a pink baseball hat over her long black hair, but it was definitely her.

Eddie Clarke was Seattle's billionaire philanthropist, best known for founding a leading pharmaceutical company. He'd never been married, and he and Alana's budding relationship was captured frequently on the gossip pages. In the last month, Cora had seen photos of them having dinner in New York and holding hands on a beach in the Caribbean. Cora was a little surprised that Alana would be flying commercial, even though she was in first class. Although, crossing the Pacific would be a long way to go in a private plane.

"Excuse me."

Cora turned her head as Alana grabbed the attention of the first-class flight attendant as she walked past their seats. The attendant moved toward Alana.

"I said *sparkling* water. Not still." Alana eyed her bottled water with a look of disgust.

"I'm so sorry," the attendant said cordially. "I'll be right back with some sparkling water for you."

"You can take this," Alana called after her, raising her bottle of water in the air.

Cora watched the attendant force a smile after she turned to take Alana's bottle from her. Cora pitied the flight attendant. She would hate to have to deal with ungrateful passengers like that.

Cora had barely opened her paperback when movement out of the corner of her eye drew her attention away from the book. She looked up to see the man who'd given the book back to her after she'd dropped it, lifting his bag into the compartment above her seat. There was a slight bulge beneath his suit jacket, and Cora recognized the dark outline of a pistol on the side of his waist before he brought his arms down.

She looked away as he sat in the empty seat beside her, wondering if she'd really seen a gun.

Cora noticed a gate agent had followed him onto the plane.

"Hey, Linda." The agent pointed in the man's direction as he handed a flight attendant with a graying bob a stack of papers.

The gate agent lowered his voice after the attendant accepted the papers. Cora couldn't hear what he was telling her, but he seemed to be explaining something about her new seatmate.

"I'm Kyle," the man said, pulling on his seatbelt.

Cora turned and looked into his brown eyes. He was even more attractive up close. She guessed he was about ten years older than herself, maybe mid-forties. "I'm Cora."

She tried to focus on her book but couldn't stop wondering if the man sitting next to her was carrying a firearm. "Are you an Air Marshal or something?"

"No." He smiled. "I'm a detective. Homicide."

"Oh," she said, feeling nosy. But he didn't seem to mind.

"Are you traveling for work?" She presumed he must be if he was able to carry his firearm.

He nodded. "I've tracked a murder suspect to Honolulu. I'm hoping to apprehend him and bring him back to Seattle."

He said it casually. She supposed it was all in a day's work for him. She was surprised to feel she had relaxed a bit. It was the first time that day she wasn't agonizing over her trip.

"My original flight got canceled last minute. This flight had the only open seats to Honolulu out of Seattle for the next couple of days. Fortunately, for me, they were in first class," he added. "You on vacation?"

"Um. No." She wasn't sure how to explain the purpose of her trip to this good-looking stranger. But he appeared to be waiting for her answer. "I'm going to Pago Pago—in Samoa. On behalf of my late husband. He's being honored for his relief efforts there. They've named a school after him. The community is having a ceremony to pay tribute to his contribution."

"Wow. He sounds like a great man. You said *late* husband? I'm sorry."

"Thank you. He was."

The first-class flight attendant leaned over their seats. Her tightly-curled blond hair was pulled into a high ponytail. "Can I get you two something to drink before we take off?" She had a slight accent which Cora guessed was eastern European. Her shiny name tag read *Mila*.

Cora shot a glance across the aisle at Alana, who grimaced while sipping her sparkling water. "I'll have a bottled water."

"I'll take coffee," the detective said.

28

Mila returned with their drinks less than a minute later. "If you need anything else just let me know."

"I could get used to this," Kyle said as the flight attendant turned across the aisle.

"Excuse me, ma'am. But you can't get up now. We're about to take off."

Cora's gaze drifted past the detective as he sipped his coffee. Alana was already out of her seat. She rolled her eyes at the flight attendant.

"I have to pee!" she yelled.

"Ma'am, I need you to take your seat so we can prepare for takeoff." The pleasantries were gone from the attendant's voice.

Alana fell back into her seat. "I should've flown private," she said, loud enough for the whole first-class cabin to hear.

The flight attendant turned away from Alana's dramatics, and Cora noticed that this time, it was Mila who rolled her eyes.

Kyle turned to Cora and smiled, and she tried to suppress a laugh at the woman's outburst. "I think that's Alana Garcia," she said quietly to the detective.

"Who's that?"

"Eddie Clarke's new girlfriend," she whispered.

He nodded. "Oh, right. I've seen her with him in the news."

The cabin went dark. Its bright lights were replaced only by illuminating strips on either side of the aisle floor and emergency exit signs. The aircraft's circulating fan turned off, creating a noticeable silence.

"That can't be good," a male voice said from the row behind them.

Cora opened her window shade to allow more natural light into the dark cabin.

"This flight's off to a great start," Alana said across the aisle.

"Ladies and gentlemen..." a male voice came over the PA system. "This is your captain from up in the flight deck. It appears one of the ground crew pulled our external power cord before we had started up our auxiliary power unit. Our auxiliary power should be coming on here in the next few minutes and then we will push back from the Jetway. We appreciate your patience."

Cora opened the cap of her water bottle, spilling some onto her lap as she put it to her lips. Kyle handed her the napkin the flight attendant had given him. His biceps were obvious though the sleeve of his suit.

"Thanks," Cora said, feeling herself blush. "I'm a little nervous. It's the first time I've left my children since my husband died."

"That's understandable," Kyle said.

"I've never been nervous to fly before," she said. "My dad is an airline pilot. Retired now. But I've been flying my whole life. Even took flying lessons in college."

"Are you a private pilot?" The detective tilted his head.

"Oh, no," she waved her hand dismissively in front of her. "I quit before I could solo. I just got too busy with nursing school. But my dad let me fly a 737 in the simulator with him a few times."

He nodded graciously, and Cora felt a flush of embarrassment. Why was she telling this complete stranger her life story? His eyes were kind, and he didn't seem to mind. She looked out the window, still wondering why she had overshared.

"I'm a nervous flier too," he said.

Cora turned toward him. "Really?"

He grinned. "Well, no. But I thought that might make you feel better."

Cora smiled, appreciating his sense of humor. She didn't know any detectives, but she hadn't expected someone who investigated murder to seem so lighthearted. And kind.

She glanced at the worn-in leather-bound book he'd placed on his lap when he sat down.

"*The Count of Monte Cristo*," he said after following her gaze. "The greatest revenge story ever told."

"I didn't know homicide detectives read literary classics."

He grinned. "Only the good ones."

She couldn't help but smile at him. "I see." She noticed he wasn't wearing a wedding ring. Sensing he caught her stare, she turned away. There was a strange flutter in her chest that she hadn't felt since she and Wesley were dating.

The cabin lights flicked on. At the same time, the hum of the circulating fan returned.

The pilot's voice came over the Intercom. "Flight attendants, please prepare for departure and crosscheck."

CHAPTER SIX

Alana's eyes followed the first-class flight attendant with disdain as the blonde woman moved toward the galley. The plane went over a bump on the taxiway, and Alana gritted her teeth from the pressure in her bladder. She tore her eyes away from the attendant and looked out the window beyond the empty seat next to her.

Alana had purchased her ticket to visit her sister in Hawaii as soon as she had found out that Maria was pregnant. She couldn't wait to meet her two-week-old niece. Eddie had offered to charter her a private plane to Hawaii, but Alana prided herself on making her own money. As the vice president of the largest investment firm on the west coast, she had plenty. Plus, a privately chartered plane to visit her sister seemed excessive. Until now.

She hadn't planned on being pregnant herself for her trip across the Pacific, dealing with an aching bladder, waves of nausea, and a controlling bitch for a flight attendant. What she would give for the comforts of a private jet. She bit her lip, wondering if Eddie had found the ultrasound photo she'd left for him.

She pulled her phone out of her sweatshirt. No new messages or missed calls. He probably hadn't seen the ultrasound yet. When she'd left for the airport, Eddie was consumed with preparing for an important meeting with his board of directors and some high-up government officials he was hosting at his home that evening. She knew him well enough to know he was probably going for a swim in the indoor lap pool to calm his nerves before the meeting.

"Excuse me, ma'am."

Alana lifted her eyes from her phone screen at the flight attendant's annoying voice. She had come to a stop in the aisle beside her seat.

"Please make sure your phone is on airplane mode."

Alana let her phone drop to her lap. "When can I use the Wi-Fi?"

"I'm sorry, but we don't offer Wi-Fi at this time on our flights over the Pacific." But she didn't look sorry at all.

Alana's jaw fell open. "Even in first class?" She was hoping to send Eddie a WhatsApp during the flight to see if he found her ultrasound photo.

"That's right." The flight attendant lingered in the aisle while Alana begrudgingly switched her iPhone to airplane mode.

"Done." Alana waved her phone in the air before she slipped it back into her sweatshirt pocket and looked up at the platinum blonde. She noticed her name tag read *Mila*. "Don't you need to sit down for takeoff, *Mila*?"

Alana was aware of how bitchy she sounded as she smiled smugly at the woman standing over her. But Mila was being unreasonable. Alana definitely could've had time to go to the bathroom.

Without a word, the attendant moved to the front of first class. Alana leaned back against her leather seat. *Only six more hours.* She hoped Eddie would be as happy as she was about her pregnancy. Once he got over the shock, just like she did.

Mila took her seat at the front of the cabin. The plane turned onto the runway. Alana closed her eyes as the aircraft increased in speed, trying not to think of her bursting bladder. Instead, she tried to focus on the positive: she might not be flying private, but at least she wasn't crammed in like cattle with the general public in the back.

CHAPTER SEVEN

Detective Kyle Adams tapped the screen on the seat in front of him. The map showed their flight in the middle of the Pacific, just over halfway to Honolulu. He stretched his legs, enjoying the ample leg room in his first-class seat and closed his eyes.

With his homicide partner away on his honeymoon, Kyle was exhausted from working his recent case solo. A missing persons case had turned into a homicide investigation when a young woman's remains were found buried in her boyfriend's backyard in West Seattle, two weeks after he'd reported her missing. Only the remains were not those of his missing girlfriend, but a teenage runaway who'd gone missing eight years earlier.

When the boyfriend found out investigators were searching his residence, he quickly boarded a flight to Honolulu. During the search, Kyle had also found traces of blood in his garage. But the missing girlfriend still hadn't been located. Kyle knew the chances of her being found alive at this point were next to nothing.

Kyle's partner, Detective Blake Stephenson, was meeting him in Honolulu on his way back from his honeymoon in Tahiti. Kyle couldn't wait to see the look on the boyfriend's face when they showed up to arrest him at his Hawaiian hideout. That sonofabitch. And, hopefully, they could get him to tell them what he'd done with his girlfriend's body.

Kyle heard his plate shake atop his tray table before his fork fell onto his lap. He opened his eyes as the Intercom pinged and the captain's voice filled the aircraft.

"Ladies and gentlemen, we're experiencing some unexpected turbulence. Please remain in your seats with your seatbelts fastened until we announce that it's safe to move about the cabin."

The pretty woman on his left flashed him a nervous smile. His heart went out to her. She was much too young to be a widow.

Cora looked out the window, and he admired her soft dark curls before he turned away. Too bad she was way out of his league.

"You're into revenge, then?"

When he looked at Cora, she nodded toward the large book on his lap.

"Oh." He brushed a finger over *The Count of Monte Cristo's* cracked leather cover. "I guess maybe a little. Probably comes from working homicide."

She nodded before turning back to the window. Kyle looked down at the book. *Was* he into revenge? If so, it really wasn't a consequence of the job.

He'd been filled with bitterness ever since his divorce. Even though years had passed, his heart remained hardened. He knew it wasn't healthy, and the only thing it had done was keep him from moving on.

It was time to let it go. Although, that was easier said than done. Kyle leaned his head back against his seat. Sleep overtook him almost as soon as he closed his eyes.

CHAPTER EIGHT

Eddie was out of breath when he climbed out of his lap pool. He looked out the window as he reached for his towel. It had been a clear day, and the downtown Seattle skyline was visible on the other side of Lake Washington.

He checked the time on his phone. He had just enough time for a quick shower before his board of directors and government officials started arriving for dinner. He wrapped his towel around his waist and stepped into the elevator, pressing the button for the third floor. He thought about the pitch he was planning to present to the heads of NASA and the Space Force.

Even though there was nothing on the market to compete with his product, he still needed to be convincing. Clarke Pharmaceuticals had spent nearly one hundred million in research over the last decade to develop this groundbreaking drug. And maximizing his profits was dependent on him delivering a convincing pitch. He smiled to himself, knowing the rewards of this meeting going well could be exorbitant.

His phone rang when he got off on the third floor. He expected it to be one of his staff letting him know the board and guests had arrived, but he didn't recognize the fifteen-digit number.

He lifted the phone to his ear as he walked through his expansive master suite. "Hello?"

"Alana's flight has been hijacked."

Eddie stopped in the middle of the room. The voice sounded computerized. A chill ran down his spine.

"You will tell the world what you've done if you want her to live. Otherwise, Alana will go down with the rest of the passengers on the plane. You have one hour. If you go to the police, she will die."

"Who is this?" Eddie yelled into the phone. But it was too late. The call had ended. It was obvious it was a recording anyway.

Alana should've been more than halfway to Hawaii by now. It had to be a prank. Someone wanting to sink his company.

A message chimed on his screen. It was from the same number. He opened it and drew in a sharp breath. A small, slightly grainy photo of Alana sitting in first class filled the screen.

Another message followed, this time only text.

If you want Alana to live, you will post a video on ALL your social media accounts and Clarke Pharmaceuticals website saying the following: I am guilty of criminal misconduct including fraud and sexually assaulting several of my former employees. I built my company, Clarke Pharmaceuticals, upon lies and false pretenses. Due to the extent of my own corruption, I am stepping down from CEO and resigning from the company. More details will follow as I intend to tell my full story to the major media outlets.

Eddie clenched his jaw. There was no way he was saying that on social media. Even if it were true. *Especially* since it was true. He tried calling the number, but an automated message told him the number had been disconnected.

Nevertheless, Eddie bit his lip and checked the news. There was nothing about a hijacking. He used his phone to turn on the large flat screen on the opposite wall. The local six o'clock news was on, and Eddie turned up the volume. Again, no mention of a hijacking. He muted the TV and called Alana, but of course, her phone went straight to voicemail.

"Alana, it's me. Call me when you land."

He had offered to charter a plane for her to go visit her sister in Hawaii, but she'd already bought the ticket before they started dating and refused to cancel it. She was completely opposite to all his previous girlfriends. She made her own money, and he'd always admired her independence. This was the first time he resented her for it.

He entered his marble bathroom and set his phone on the counter next to the ultrasound photo Alana had left for him. He'd been on cloud nine since she surprised him with the news that afternoon. Now, he felt sick at the thought of anything happening to Alana and their unborn child.

He reached for his phone again and did an Internet search for *plane hijacked*. There were no recent results. He typed *missing plane*. Again, there was nothing relevant. He found Alana's flight number and typed it into the search bar. The top result showed that it was en route.

He should call the police. Let them track the call. But then there would be an investigation. Possibly even a public one. His phone rang in his hand, making him jump. It was his assistant.

He stared at the ultrasound photo as he put the phone to his ear. "Yeah?"

"The board and your guests from Washington are here. I've seated them for dinner."

"Okay. I'll be down in fifteen minutes."

Eddie set his phone on the counter and stepped into his shower. He closed his eyes as the warm water rushed over his face from the rain shower head. By the time he turned off the water, he'd assured himself that Alana, and his baby, were fine.

This had to be an empty threat. It wasn't the first time someone had tried to get money from him through extortion. He was one of the wealthiest men in the United States.

After getting dressed, he grabbed his phone off the bathroom counter. As he walked out of his room toward the elevator, he tried to focus his thoughts on what he'd planned to say during his meeting. He pressed the call button for the elevator before reopening the grainy photo of Alana.

Who had taken it? And, if it was an empty threat, how did they have a photo of Alana on that flight? And how did they get his private cell number? Unless, it wasn't an empty threat, but a premeditated attack. He looked at the photo again, wondering if it could've been an old picture. But he recognized the pink baseball hat she wore with her long black hair cascading beneath it. She'd just bought the hat, and she'd been wearing it when she left for the airport that afternoon.

He searched her flight number again as the elevator doors opened. Still nothing in the news. It struck him again that he should call the police. Could he prevent a hijacking from happening if he did?

But he had no reason to believe the phone call and text message he'd received. It was practically impossible to hijack a plane after the September 11 attacks, he assured himself. He had no reason to panic. Or do anything as catastrophic as posting an incriminating confession video online which could prompt a police investigation.

Eddie stepped into the elevator, thinking there was something he *could* do. He quickly found the number for Justin in his phone contacts. The elevator doors closed as he lifted the phone to his ear. He was relieved when Justin answered after the first ring.

"Hey, boss."

"Hey, I need a favor."

"Sure."

"I need you to trace a phone number for me. I need any and every bit of information you can get."

"No problem," Justin said without hesitation. It wasn't the first time he'd done unconventional work for Eddie outside his official job description.

"Thank you. I'll text you the number."

"All right."

Eddie let his phone fall to his side after he sent the text. There. He'd done *something*. Justin was the best IT expert money could buy. If there was any information to find about the number that threatened him, he would find it.

Now, Eddie could have peace of mind while he landed the biggest contract of his career.

A new message lit up his phone screen when the elevator doors opened. Eddie lifted his phone in slow motion, mentally preparing himself for another threat. *The board is waiting.*

The tension in his muscles relaxed. He tucked his phone into his pocket without replying to his assistant and stepped onto the second floor of his home. He ran a hand through his damp hair. It was time to do what he did best.

CHAPTER NINE

Kyle's mouth was dry when he opened his eyes. He wasn't sure how long he'd been asleep. He'd allowed himself to drift off not long after finally finishing *The Count of Monte Cristo*, relishing the accomplishment. The first-class cabin was quiet aside from the constant drone from the engines. He checked the map on his small screen. It looked like they were over an hour from Honolulu.

Cora was still reading her paperback novel in the seat beside him. He noticed the fasten seatbelt sign had been turned off. A soft click interrupted the silence and Kyle watched the cockpit door swing open.

One of the pilots emerged and nodded at the flight attendant making coffee in the galley before he stepped into the first-class lavatory. Kyle took a drink from his water bottle as the man sitting in front of him stood from his seat. The man moved to the front of the cabin and opened the overhead compartment.

Kyle watched him rifle through the compartment and wondered why he would've put his carry-on so far away from his seat. But, then again, it was almost a full flight. Maybe there wasn't room in his overhead compartment.

The lavatory door opened, and Kyle saw the pilot say something to the flight attendant as he moved past her. A smile escaped her lips before he lifted the phone beside the cockpit door. There was an audible click, and the pilot replaced the phone and opened the door.

The passenger stopped rifling through the overhead bin at the front of first class and turned toward the pilot with his arm outstretched. Kyle spotted the gun in the man's hand at the same time he fired a shot at the pilot's head.

The sound from the blast boomed through the cabin. The pilot's blood splattered onto the flight attendant's face. She screamed as he fell to the floor at her feet. She leaned against the cockpit door as the armed passenger charged toward her.

"Move!" he yelled, pointing his gun at her face.

The attendant put her hands up in surrender and slowly stepped away from the door. She closed her eyes as the man moved toward her, as if bracing herself for a bullet to the head.

Kyle reached for his firearm as the man across the aisle from him in the next row jumped out of his seat. The man lifted a pistol in his right hand, pointing the weapon toward the other passengers as he pivoted toward the back of the plane.

"Stay in your seats!" the man shouted over the screeching passengers.

A male flight attendant charged him from the main cabin. The hijacker's gun went off a split-second before Kyle fired a round into his chest. A bullet to the head sent the flight attendant to the floor. The hijacker fired a second round as he recoiled from the bullet to his chest, shooting another flight attendant behind a drink cart before he fell backward into Alana Garcia's lap.

She screamed and pushed him off her, into the aisle. The man's gun went off again, sending a bullet through the ceiling of the aircraft as Kyle fired another round into the hijacker's head.

Kyle's ears rung from the gunfire in the small space. The sharp hiss of air escaping out the aircraft through the bullet hole above his head was barely audible over the passengers' screams.

Blood seeped onto the thin carpet from the hijacker's bullet wounds. His eyes stared blankly at the ceiling. Kyle kicked the gun away from his lifeless hand when he felt Cora's hand on his arm.

"The other man is inside the cockpit!" she exclaimed.

Kyle leapt over the dead man's body. The first-class flight attendant stood frozen in shock next to the cockpit with her back against the wall. Another shot rang out from inside the flight deck. The cockpit door was ajar, and Kyle's eyes locked with the hijacker as he started to pull the door closed. Kyle lunged for it, and the hijacker raised his gun at the detective. Kyle ducked as the hijacker pulled the trigger, the blast resounding through the cabin.

Kyle returned fire. The hijacker shielded himself behind the bulletproof door before poking his gun through the cracked doorway again. Kyle dove forward and closed his grip around his assailant's gun wrist. He shoved the door into the hijacker's arm.

The gun went off again as Kyle slammed the hijacker's hand into the wall, sending another bullet into the wall of the plane.

"Get down!" Kyle yelled to the passengers behind him, thinking particularly of the woman sitting next to him.

Kyle shoved the steel door into the hijacker's arm. He felt the man's grip loosen on the weapon and yanked it out of his hold. Kyle wedged his foot behind the door, letting the hijacker's gun fall to the floor as the man tried to pull the door closed.

The hijacker let go of the door and closed his hand around Kyle's throat. Kyle gasped for air and lifted his pistol. The hijacker closed his grip around Kyle's wrist, forcing his hand holding the gun into the wall behind him. Kyle wheezed as he tried unsuccessfully to draw in a breath of air.

He gritted his teeth as he fought to lift his arm from under the hijacker's hold. The man was stronger than he looked. Kyle pressed his open palm into the man's face as he slowly lifted the barrel of his gun and pulled the trigger.

The hijacker released his grip from Kyle's neck as the bullet entered his torso. The plane lurched from a gust of turbulence, and both men fell to the aircraft floor. The hijacker reached for his gun that lay next to him when another shot rang off. Kyle got to his knees as he watched his attacker go still. Blood oozed from both bullet wounds in his chest.

The first-class flight attendant stood over the dying man, her shaking outstretched arms holding the other hijacker's pistol. Kyle brought his hand to his throat as he stood to his feet. He wanted to ask why she didn't pull the trigger when the hijacker was squeezing the life out of him, but Kyle could see she was in shock.

"There's a hole in the plane!" someone yelled.

The shrill hiss from the bullet holes in the first-class cabin was audible over the shrieks coming from the passengers in the back. Kyle picked the hijacker's gun up from the floor and moved toward the main cabin.

He put up his hands and spoke toward the passengers in the back. "It's okay. If the shots had depressurized the airplane, the oxygen masks would've dropped."

He noticed Cora was bent over the male flight attendant who'd been shot in the head.

"But we should cover up those holes," Kyle added.

He turned to find the first-class flight attendant still at the front of the plane. She hadn't moved from where he'd last seen her. Her eyes were fixed on the hijacker bleeding out on the floor. Kyle moved slowly toward the flight attendant.

"Hey," he spoke softly as he glanced at her name tag.

She tore her eyes away from the man she'd shot and met his gaze.

"Mila, we need to plug those bullet holes in the side of the plane. Is there something we could use for that?" They were lucky none of them went through a window.

"Um." She closed her eyes. "We have tape in our medical kit."

"Good. Let's try that."

He turned for the cockpit, knowing with a sinking feeling what he was about to find. He pushed open the cockpit door and saw the captain slumped over the controls. The back of his hair was matted with blood.

Kyle took a deep breath and stepped out of the flight deck. Cora had come up to the front and was bent over the copilot. She pressed two fingers against the side of his neck. She looked up when Kyle stepped over them.

"I'm a nurse," she said. "He doesn't have a pulse. Neither do the two flight attendants who were shot." She nodded toward the man who lay in the middle of the aisle beside their seats.

"The guy you shot back there is dead."

She bent over the hijacker at their feet, feeling his neck for a pulse. She looked up at Kyle. "They're both gone."

Kyle heard a baby crying in the main cabin. Passengers were starting to flood first class. They were pushing each other to try and see what was happening. Several were yelling hysterically.

Kyle headed back toward his seat, where a couple passengers were helping the first-class flight attendant tape over the bullet holes. The piece of tape they stuck to the wall was quickly sucked out the hole. The loud hissing returned.

"My dad told me they used wet toilet paper in the Air Force to plug small holes in their planes."

Kyle turned to see Cora beside him.

Mila raised her eyebrows. "Toilet paper?"

Cora nodded. "Yeah, they would get it wet and wad it up against the hole. Then the end would get sucked outside and freeze to seal the leaking air."

A male passenger tossed the medical tape onto a seat. "It's worth a try. I'll go get some."

Kyle and Cora stepped aside for him to move past them. Kyle stepped toward Mila and put his hand on her shoulder.

"You need to get on the Intercom and tell everyone to calm down. The hijackers are dead. We need them to stop panicking."

She turned toward him. "Okay."

"Is that the pilot?" one of the passengers from the back screamed, seeing the co-pilot's body at the front of first class.

"Please!" Kyle put both hands in the air. "We need everyone to return to their seats."

He turned toward Mila as she pulled the Intercom from the wall. "Try not to alarm everyone," he said to her in a low voice. He took a step toward her over the dead hijacker. "But we need to know if there's anyone on board who can fly a plane."

CHAPTER TEN

Asha set her phone on the counter after refreshing the news page and stirred the spiced rice dish atop her coiled stove top. The two-bedroom apartment was a few miles south of the airport, which was close enough to hear the large jets as they took off. A constant reminder of what she'd done.

She was about to check the news again when she heard her husband and daughters come through their apartment door.

Aaden looked startled when he saw her in their small kitchen. "I thought you were at work."

"Mommy!" her two girls ran into the kitchen with their arms out.

Asha bent down and pulled them both into a tight embrace. Their coats were sleek with rain. Aaden unzipped his jacket, waiting for her answer.

"I was," Asha said. "But I came home early. I wasn't feeling well."

"Sorry." Aaden looked concerned.

She'd worried he'd be upset, even question her. But she realized that was a fabrication from her guilty conscience.

She hated lying to him, but it wasn't far from the truth. She'd been so sick to her stomach after planting that gun on the flight that she thought she might throw up.

"That's okay. I'm starting to feel better." Asha turned to her girls. "Why don't you two get started on your homework? Dinner will be ready soon."

After the girls ran out of the kitchen, Asha turned back to the stove. She felt Aaden move in behind her.

"Is that Bariis Iskukaris?"

"Yes." She'd needed something to take her mind off what she'd done. The flight was due to land in Honolulu in less than an hour and a half. But there still wasn't anything on the news.

"It smells amazing. You must not be feeling *that* bad if you're feeling up to making my favorite dish."

She turned to see him smiling. If you only knew what I've done.

"I thought it might make me feel better," she lied.

She couldn't stop wondering if the rest of her family was dead. She'd had no more messages from the terrorists. Hopefully, they knew she'd picked up the 'package' yesterday. And, by now, the terrorists should've known she'd planted the gun on the plane.

She'd called the number that had sent her the video, but it was disconnected. And she didn't dare contact her family in their rural village, afraid she might risk their safety by calling them.

"I'm sure it will." Aaden kissed her lightly on the temple before he stepped out of the kitchen.

Asha gave the rice a stir before she lifted her phone from the counter and searched the news again. Still nothing.

"How come you don't make this more often?"

"Because it's a lot of work," Aaden answered their daughter.

The girls' plates were nearly empty, and Aaden was already on his second helping of their native dish. Asha's plate was still untouched as she stared at the table.

She felt Aaden's hand on her arm. "Asha? You okay? Maybe you should go lie down."

The plane was supposed to arrive in Hawaii in an hour. Last she checked, there was still no news of a plane going missing or being hijacked. But maybe it wouldn't make the news until it didn't arrive in Honolulu. From what she'd read online, Pacific Air flights didn't have Wi-Fi over the Pacific. No cell service either. So, just because it hadn't made the news yet didn't mean something hadn't happened to that flight.

There were probably children on it. She thought of a mother holding her screaming child as the plane crashed into the ocean. Asha pushed out her chair and stood from the table. She had no control over what happened to her extended family. She'd done what was demanded of her.

Maybe there was something that could still be done for the people on that flight. And she needed to be able to live with herself for the rest of her life.

"I forgot there was something I needed to do this evening. An errand. I'll be back later."

"What errand?" Aaden turned around in his seat as Asha grabbed her purse off the kitchen counter.

Asha avoided his eye contact. She couldn't tell him what she'd done in front of their girls. What would she say? Plus, there wasn't time.

"Halima is sick. I forgot I promised her that I'd bring over some groceries."

"What's wrong with her?" Aaden asked.

"Sorry, I have to hurry." She was almost to the front door. "I'll tell you more when I get home."

She could only hope he forgave her when he found out.

CHAPTER ELEVEN

The flight attendant lowered the Intercom's mouthpiece. "I was a helicopter pilot in the Kosovo Security Force before I immigrated to America," she said to Kyle. "But I've never flown anything like this."

"Okay. That's good," Kyle said. *Why hadn't she said anything sooner?* But she *had* just shot a man and looked to be in shock. "We should also check if there's another pilot on board that could help you. Maybe there's even an airline pilot on the flight."

She nodded and lifted the receiver to her lips. "Ladies and gentlemen. I want to ask everyone to please remain calm and return to your seats." She took a deep breath. Kyle noticed her hand was shaking. She still had the pistol in her other hand at her side. "There appeared to be two hijackers on board in first class, but they are both dead."

Kyle turned back for the cockpit as the passengers seemed to all call out panicked questions at once. If the flight attendant was a helicopter pilot, he felt fairly confident that with some instruction, she should be able to land the plane. And, maybe, they'd be lucky enough to have another pilot on board.

He reached for the headset in the empty seat next to the dead captain. Every few seconds, a *ping* came over the speakers above the pilot's seats. He slid the earpieces over his ears and stared at the control panel. To someone who'd never flown a plane before, the number of screens and controls was overwhelming.

A staticky voice came through the headset immediately. "Pacific Air 385. Oakland."

He scanned the row of screens on the control panel. "This is Flight 385," he said. "Can you hear me?"

Another *ping* filled the cockpit. "Pacific Air 385. Oakland Center," the voice repeated.

Kyle moved his eyes to the yoke and found a switch behind the word *MIC* on the left-hand side. He held it down with his thumb while he spoke. "This is Flight 385. Do you read me?"

"We read you, Pacific Air 385. What's your position?"

"I'm not sure what our position is, but we've been hijacked. The hijackers are dead, but so are the pilots."

"Pacific Air 385, can you repeat that and confirm that you have been hijacked?"

The overhead *ping* had stopped.

"Yes, we have been *hijacked*. The hijackers *and* the pilots are dead."

"Roger that. Are you still under any duress?"

"No. But—"

Kyle turned toward Mila when she stepped into the cockpit.

"Are there any other pilots on board?" the air traffic controller said into Kyle' ears.

"The first-class flight attendant is an ex-military helicopter pilot." Kyle let go of the *MIC* switch and lifted the headset away from his ear. "Did you ask if there's any other pilots on board?"

Mila shook her head. "Not yet. But I can make the announcement from in here."

Kyle pulled the headset back over his ear and pressed the *MIC* switch on the yoke. "We're just about to make an announcement to see if there's any other pilots on board."

"Roger that. If there's no airline pilot on board, I'll get a pilot on the radio to talk you through the landing. In the meantime, can you give me your coordinates?"

"Um. Yeah. Just a second. I have to find where that's displayed. Maybe I should have her tell you."

Kyle lowered the headset and turned to the flight attendant.

"If there's no airline pilot on board, they're going to get a pilot on the radio to talk you through the landing." He pulled off the headset and handed it to her. "Here. They need to know our coordinates."

She still had the gun in her hand.

"Do you want me to take that?" He pointed to the weapon.

Mila accepted the headset and looked down at her other hand holding the gun. "I think I'd like to keep it." Her eyes moved to the back of the captain's bloody head slumped over the controls.

Kyle turned and followed her gaze.

"What if there's still a hijacker on board?" she asked. "I mean, how do we know those were the only two? And how did they get *two guns* on the plane?"

"I don't know. But if it makes you feel better, keep the gun."

Mila's eyes remained fixed on the dead captain. "We need to get him off the controls for the landing."

"Okay." Kyle squatted beside the pilot.

"Do you want some help?"

"No, I got it."

Mila put on the headset. She climbed into the co-pilot's seat as Kyle carefully pulled the captain away from the instrument panel. He unbuckled the captain's seatbelt and noticed there was no exit wound from the bullet that entered the back of his head, which was probably a good thing. If the bullet had exited, it would've gone through the controls.

Kyle grabbed the man by his armpits and pulled him from his seat. He guessed the captain weighed about 200 pounds. Thanks to his daily weightlifting regimen, the detective was able to lift him out single-handedly. He heard Mila read their coordinates to the air traffic controller.

There wasn't much floor space to move him within the cockpit. Even though the passengers knew the pilots were dead, he didn't want to alarm them further by dragging the captain's body into the main cabin. Kyle carefully lifted his body into the tight space of the jump seat directly behind the captain's seat. There wasn't enough leg room to squeeze the man's legs in, so Kyle left them protruding into the middle of the cockpit.

"Ladies and gentlemen," he heard Mila say, "this is Mila from the flight deck. I'm the first-class flight attendant, and I have experience as a military pilot. If there are any other pilots on board, please come forward and assist me in the landing. Come up to the front and call into the cockpit. Thank you."

Kyle buckled the pilot's body into the seat as Mila made the announcement. Once the captain was secured in the seat, he closed the man's eyelids out of respect. A phone rang in the middle of the cockpit, interrupting the somber moment.

Kyle felt a wave of relief. It had only been a minute since Mila's announcement. Hopefully, the call meant there was an airline pilot on board. He turned toward Mila as she lifted the receiver.

"This is Mila."

Kyle waited expectantly as she listened to the other end of the call.

"Okay," she finally said. "Tell the passengers that we have an experienced pilot who's going to land the plane with the help of an airline captain over the radio. And they can help by staying calm."

Kyle's earlier relief dissipated. Mila must be the only pilot on board. She turned to him after hanging up the receiver.

"That was Linda, the other flight attendant. No pilots have come forward, and the passengers are panicking."

Kyle told himself it could be worse. There could've been no pilots on board. With the help of an airline pilot over the radio, the odds should be good that Mila could successfully land the plane.

Mila still had her headset off one of her ears. He watched her flip a switch on the control panel.

"How come you're working as a flight attendant when you're a pilot?"

She answered without turning around. "I'm still working on getting my commercial pilot's license in the U.S. But it takes money. And time. Meanwhile, I have to the pay the bills."

Kyle nodded, even though she wasn't looking at him. Before getting up, he said a prayer for the captain. Then he said one for Mila, who had all their lives in her hands.

CHAPTER TWELVE

Asha rung her hands together atop the metal table in the small interview room at the SeaTac Police Department. Two detectives, a man and a woman, sat across from her. When she'd arrived and told the officer at the front desk that she planted a gun on a plane, he'd looked at her like she was crazy. Until she showed him the video she had received on her phone.

She'd been ushered into a small room on the second floor with one-way mirrored glass on one wall. After they had read her Miranda rights, the last half hour was spent telling these detectives everything that had happened in the past forty-eight hours.

"And the gun was loaded?" the man asked.

Asha was too distraught to remember their names.

"That you put on the plane?" he added, as if Asha had forgotten what gun he was asking about.

"I don't know. I assumed so." She looked between the detectives. "I—I didn't check."

They stared back at her.

"It felt like it was," she continued. "It felt heavy for such a small gun. But I was so focused on what might happen to my family if I *didn't* put the gun on the plane, I didn't bother to check. Plus, I would've had to Google how to even do that."

Asha looked into the man's intelligent eyes.

"Could I have my phone back?" she asked.

The detective shook his head. "Not now. It's been taken as evidence."

"But you'll save my family? In Somalia?" she asked.

"We will look into what happened and see if there's anything our government can do," the man said.

"*Look into it?*" Asha stared across the table at the detective who'd responded as if she'd made a customer service complaint. "But I came forward." She placed her hand on her chest and jumped to her feet. "You have to help them!"

The woman held up her hand. "Please, sit down."

Asha remained standing. "I came here for all those people on that flight, but also for my *family*." She choked back her tears. "Please! You have to do something for them. Before it's too late!" She looked back and forth between their blank stares. "This is America! You have the power to do whatever you want. You have military over there, right? Near there, I know you do. If those terrorists find out I've gone to the police, they'll kill them all! You have to save them."

The door to the interview room opened. All three of them turned to the man in the doorway who held a cell phone in his hand.

"We've just received confirmation that Pacific Air Flight 385 has been hijacked," he said to the detectives.

Asha felt like she might throw up. *How many lives had been taken?*

"The flight has made contact with Oakland Center, the air traffic control center that monitors all flights on this side of the Pacific. The passengers helped regain control of the plane. They claim that the hijackers are dead. But so are both of the pilots."

Asha watched the detectives exchange a look. "We need to call the FBI," the woman said.

"I already did," the man in the doorway said. "Two agents are on their way." He shifted his gaze to Asha. "They'll want to speak to you." He turned back to the detectives. "They've also sent units to the address where she picked up the gun. And the federal prosecutor is on her way here."

Asha hung her head. The pilots were dead because of her. She wondered if they had someone who could land the plane, but knew she had no right to ask after what she'd done. The male detective stood up and moved around the table. He pulled a pair of handcuffs from his pocket.

"Asha Farar, you are under arrest for carrying a concealed firearm without a permit and carrying a firearm into a restricted area." He secured one cuff around her wrist and the other to the table. "And once the FBI and federal prosecutor arrive, you'll likely also be charged with providing material support for terrorism and aiding and abetting terrorists. They might also charge you with conspiracy. But, since you're cooperating, and you acted while your family was under duress, I would imagine the prosecutor might offer some leniency as far as your sentencing goes."

Asha lifted her head when he had finished. "What about my family?"

Across the table, the female detective pursed her lips. "Like we said, we will pass the information about your family on to the appropriate authorities, but it's not our department. They are out of our control."

"I need to call my husband," she said as the man closed the door.

"You can call him after we book you. But that won't be until after you speak with the FBI."

Asha looked away from the woman as she spoke and stared at the metal table. This was a mistake. It was too late to stop the hijacking, and the police weren't even going to help her family. It might already be too late for them, too.

She would go to jail for what she'd done. Leave her daughters without a mother. She was afraid to ask for how long. And for what? It had been too late to right her wrong.

Asha stared at the Styrofoam cup of water the detectives had set in front of her at the start of the interview. "I think I'd like a lawyer."

The detective stood from her chair on the other side of the table. "I think that's a good idea."

CHAPTER THIRTEEN

"Ladies and gentlemen, we have an experienced pilot on board who is going to land the plane with the help of an airline captain over the radio. But we need your help by remaining calm. Everything is under control. I'm asking that everyone return to their seats until we land in Honolulu."

Cora stepped over the dead hijacker and got back in her seat as the flight attendant requested. Now that the bullet holes were sealed, there was nothing to drown out the hysterical outcries from panicked passengers. Two men from the row behind her lifted the hijacker's body and moved it to the floor of the empty front row.

Cora leaned her head against her seat and closed her eyes as a baby let out a high-pitched cry in the back of the plane. She glanced at the empty seat next to her while the remaining first-class passengers took their seats. The detective hadn't returned from the cockpit, and Cora wondered if he would stay there until they landed.

She hadn't seen anyone go into the cockpit other than Kyle and the first-class flight attendant. Was one of them the experienced pilot who was going to land the plane?

Kyle hadn't said anything about being a pilot, so maybe it was the flight attendant. Unless there'd been another pilot in one of the jump seats.

She felt irresponsible and overcome by guilt for leaving her children when she was the only parent they had left. She was still in shock of what had happened. Cora bit her lip and opened her eyes. The two men passed by her seat again, this time carrying the body of the male flight attendant.

She watched Alana Garcia buckle her seatbelt across the aisle with shaking hands. Alana's face had gone pale. Her terrified eyes met Cora's for a brief moment before Alana looked away.

Cora thought back to what she'd seen right after the hijacking. Maybe it wasn't what it had looked like. She wondered if any of the other passengers had seen it. If they did, no one had said anything.

She needed to tell someone. She needed to tell Kyle.

A woman's scream erupted from the middle of the plane.

"We need a doctor!" a male voice called out. "Is anyone a doctor?"

Cora unbuckled her seatbelt and looked toward the rear of the plane. A man and woman were crouched over an older man lying in the aisle. She jumped up and entered the main cabin, noting that the drink cart had been cleared from the aisle. The female flight attendant's body remained on the floor, but thankfully someone had covered her bloodied head with a blanket. Cora took a large stride over her, careful not to tread on the attendant's body or the blood that had seeped onto the floor around her.

"I'm a nurse," Cora said as she got closer.

The man turned and moved so Cora could get to the man lying on the floor. She knelt in the narrow space beside him. He looked to be about seventy and was struggling to breathe. His hand clutched the left side of his chest. He was conscious, but barely. The man groaned before he drew in a sharp gasp.

"Barry!" an older woman cried on the other side of him.

"What happened?" Cora asked her.

"We were returning to our seats like the flight attendant said. He suddenly clutched his arm and fell to the floor. He passed out for a moment."

"Okay." Cora unbuttoned the top of the man's shirt, noticing the pallor of his skin.

A flight attendant rushed to their side. She looked older than Mila. Her blonde bob was speckled with gray. Cora glanced at her name tag pinned to her uniform: *Linda.*

"He needs oxygen," Cora said.

"We have a portable tank on board." Linda took careful steps over them toward the rear.

"Has he had a heart attack before?" Cora asked the woman she presumed was his wife.

She shook her head. "No."

Beads of sweat had formed on the man's forehead. Cora grabbed two pillows off the seats next to her and gently placed them under his head. She was glad to see he was still breathing, even though it was labored. She checked his pulse. It was rapid and weak.

"Does anyone have aspirin?" Cora called out to the other passengers.

"I have aspirin," a woman said.

She appeared at Cora's side a moment later and handed her a small bottle. A passenger in the row next to them handed her a bottle of water. Cora helped the man sit up. He winced and placed a hand on his chest. Cora shook out one of the pills.

"Take this," she said, helping him bring the bottle to his lips. Water spilled out the sides of his mouth as he swallowed the pill.

Cora looked up when Linda returned—empty handed—from the back.

"The oxygen tank wasn't where we normally keep it," Linda said. "I'll see if it's with our medical kit at the front."

Cora refocused her attention on the older man as Linda climbed over them. His color was worsening, and he was having trouble sitting up. She helped him lie back against the pillows.

The plane lurched downward, making Cora feel weightless for a second until the plane jolted up again. In her effort to not fall on the man lying beneath her, Cora was knocked off balance, smacking her head against the armrest of the seat behind her before she fell to the floor.

The plane hit a few more bumps as she pulled herself up from the floor, the rough turbulence serving as a reminder that they might not be far from their final moments. As she got to her knees, her eyes met with a small boy sitting next to the aisle. He looked the same age as her daughter Zoe.

Linda returned with a large black case of medical supplies. Cora was dismayed to see there was no oxygen tank. Linda knelt behind Cora and opened the medical kit.

"I checked the overhead compartments at the front, but there was no oxygen."

"Is there anywhere else it could be?" Cora asked.

Linda shook her head. "No, but I'll grab one of our flight attendant emergency bottles from the back."

Before getting up, Linda rifled through the case and started pulling supplies onto the floor. Cora watched her lift a large bag of normal saline, IV tubing, and a small first-aid kit onto the floor.

Cora leaned over to see what else was in the medical kit. "I'll take that stethoscope and blood pressure cuff."

Linda handed them to her.

Cora took his blood pressure then pulled the stethoscope away from her ears. "His pressure is low. I'm going to start an IV."

The flight attendant stepped over them to retrieve the oxygen bottle while Cora started an IV in the man's arm. After securing it with tape, she held the bag of normal saline up to the passenger sitting in the adjacent aisle seat.

"Here I need you to hold this."

Cora spiked the bag, primed the tubing, and connected it to the man's IV. She sat back on her heels and eyed the rest of the contents inside the medical kit. She recognized the brown glass bottle containing nitroglycerin.

While she was almost certain the man was having a heart attack, she couldn't confirm it without an EKG. If his blood pressure wasn't so low, she would have given him a nitroglycerin anyway. But doing so now might kill him. She'd have to wait and see if his blood pressure came up from the IV fluids.

She turned back to the man on the floor. He was still breathing, but there was a slight gray tone to his pale skin. His wife leaned over Cora's shoulder.

"Barry! Can you hear me? *Barry!*"

He didn't respond. Cora worried he was starting to slip from consciousness.

Linda returned with a green portable oxygen bottle. She turned on the bottle as Cora secured the mask around the man's nose and mouth.

"Is there an AED in there? We might need it." Cora peeked into the medical kit, noting a couple vials of emergency drugs used for cardiac arrest.

"Yes." The flight attendant pulled out a small lime-green automatic defibrillator and handed it to Cora.

It felt incredibly light, and Cora flipped it over in her hands. "Where's the batteries?"

"They should be in there," Linda said.

"Well, they're not." Cora held up the back of the defibrillator. "Are they inside the case?"

The attendant dug through the rest of its contents. "They're not here." She locked eyes with Cora. "I'm sorry. I don't know what's happened."

Cora looked at the man whose eyes had closed. Even with the oxygen, his skin was now mottled. She watched his chest rise and fall with shallow breaths.

"Barry!" his wife cried, shaking him by the shoulder.

He didn't respond.

He needed emergency room treatment. There wasn't much more Cora could do for him—unless his heart stopped. Then she could give him CPR, along with the emergency drugs. It would be at least two more hours before he would get to a hospital. If they survived the landing.

Cora tried to push the last thought from her mind and turned to the flight attendant. "Let's hope we don't need it. Is there another one of these tanks, in case this one runs out?"

Linda nodded. "There's one for each of the flight attendants."

A grim look came over Linda's face. Cora knew she was likely thinking about her two dead coworkers.

"I'll check again for the medical tank in the front," Linda added.

"Okay good."

Linda stared at the man lying on the floor. "I've never had it be missing before."

CHAPTER FOURTEEN

"What a mess."

Thomas had been the president's chief of staff for nearly four years, but this was, by far, the biggest scandal to impact the administration. Only a month from the next election.

Thomas rubbed his eyes as the press secretary refilled his coffee before pouring one for herself.

"Thank you," he said, knowing that neither of them would be getting much sleep tonight.

It was nearly midnight, and the president had gone to bed, leaving them to prepare for the next morning's press conference where they would be met with an onslaught of hostile, accusatory journalists hungry for negative press to use against their administration.

Whitney leaned against his desk and took a sip of her black coffee. Speech writers and other staffers filled the table behind them. She slipped out of one of her Ted Baker heels and stretched the ball of her foot on the woven carpet. The room's pale-yellow curtains beyond Thomas's desk seemed more familiar than those at her own house. In the six months she'd been press secretary, she felt like she'd hardly been home.

Her eyes followed Thomas's to his computer screen. A stack of papers was piled high to the side of his computer on his already-cluttered desk.

"How could we be the last to know about this?" He stared at the news article that was posted a few hours earlier.

Whitney didn't respond. Even if she had an answer, it wouldn't make a difference. All they could do now was handle the press and move on, while trying to minimize the damage this could have on the upcoming election.

A photo of the president's newly appointed Secretary of the Treasury being led out of his Georgetown mansion in handcuffs topped the article. A bold headline ran across the top of the page:

SECRETARY OF THE TREASURY ARRESTED FOR LEAKING CLASSIFIED INFO TO FEMALE ESCORT

Whitney had already read the article. The married father of four had allegedly given a female escort access to his government-issued laptop from which she leaked countless classified documents online. As well as a sex tape of her and the secretary. And the press was having a field day.

The president had fired the secretary upon his arrest, and they'd agreed to hold a press conference in the morning.

But Whitney could handle it. This was why she'd been hired. She would deny any knowledge of the current administration in the secretary's offenses, condemn what he'd done, and shut down any accusations that would suggest otherwise.

She liked Thomas, and he'd lasted longer than most chiefs of staff. But, lately, she could see the stress of the job had been eating away at him, especially with the pressure of the upcoming election. He and the president had known each other since law school. So, Thomas was taking this hard. She had overheard him and the country's leader exchanging terse words earlier that evening and knew Thomas felt responsible for advising the president to appoint the secretary a few months back.

Whitney wondered how long the president would keep Thomas around if she got re-elected. Thomas chewed his lip and read through the article. His desk phone rang, but Thomas hesitated before answering. It wouldn't be the first time the press had gotten through. Whitney watched him lift the receiver after the third ring.

"This is Thomas."

Whitney took another sip of her coffee, waiting patiently to find out who was on the other end of the line.

"*Hijacked?* Are you sure?" Thomas nearly dropped his mug onto the desk, spilling coffee onto his keyboard.

Whitney's eyes widened as Thomas stood from his seat. "Okay. I'll wake the president and call an emergency meeting in the Cabinet Room. Come as quick as you can."

Thomas slammed down the receiver and brought his hand to his forehead. He turned wearily to Whitney. "That was the Secretary of Homeland Security. A commercial airliner has been hijacked on its way to Honolulu. The hijackers have been killed, but so were the pilots. They have an ex-military pilot on board who is going to attempt an emergency landing at Honolulu airport."

Whitney raised a hand to her mouth. Thomas turned as he scurried out of the room. "Don't say anything to the press! Not yet."

She shook her head. "I won't."

CHAPTER FIFTEEN

Kyle got to his feet in the back of the cockpit. Mila was busy getting instruction through her headset at the front of the cockpit. He looked down at the dead pilot and wondered how the hijackers had gotten the guns on the plane. *Had they had help? And what was their motivation? Terrorism?*

Kyle realized they knew nothing about the two men who had murdered the pilots and tried to take over the plane. They were both middle-aged and white, and they hadn't claimed any allegiances to either a terrorist organization or militia group.

Kyle stepped out of the cockpit. They would hopefully be on the ground shortly, but he needed to start by finding out who they were.

He stopped when he got to the front of first class. The first row had been empty, and the two hijackers' bodies had been moved to the row on his left, with the copilot and male flight attendant to the row on his right. Someone had covered them with blankets from the waist up. Kyle stepped aside to make room for two passengers who were carrying the second deceased flight attendant's body to the front. A blanket slipped off her head as they pivoted, exposing a hollow bullet wound in the center of her forehead. The two men carefully placed her beside the other crew members in the front row. Kyle picked the blanket up off the floor and handed it to one of the men, who draped it over the attendant's head.

The two men returned to their seats in the row behind Kyle, and he noticed Cora was gone. The curtain was drawn, separating first class from the main cabin. He guessed the remaining flight attendant might have hoped that keeping the passengers from seeing the dead bodies that had piled up in the front of the plane would reduce the panic.

Kyle crossed the aisle and bent down next to the man who'd nearly killed him. He found a wallet in the back pocket of the man's jeans. He pulled it out and examined the driver's license. His name was Neil Kowalski, and he had a Bellevue address. He was forty-two. Kyle closed the wallet and moved to the body of the other hijacker. He found a wallet in the pocket of his cargo pants. He was Conner Bateman; forty-three and also lived in Bellevue. No photos in either of the wallets, although, Kyle realized, this was not unusual. Everyone kept photos on their phones now.

Phones. He felt the man's cargo pockets again but, surprisingly, they were all empty. He checked the other deceased man's pockets. Also empty.

Kyle sat back on his knees. It seemed unlikely they both were traveling without a phone, even if this was a suicide mission.

The curtain swung open from the main cabin and Linda briskly made her way to the front of first class. She moved straight for the open compartment where Kyle had watched one of the hijackers pull out a gun. She stood on her toes and ran her hand along the inside of the overhead bin. She withdrew a pillow and a blanket, tossing them onto the seat beneath her.

Kyle's eyes followed in the direction she'd come from. He saw Cora bent over a passenger lying in the aisle toward the middle of the plane. *Some sort of medical emergency,* Kyle thought. If only that had been the worst of their problems on this flight.

"What are you looking for?" Kyle stood up and moved toward the flight attendant.

She turned to face him. "A medical oxygen tank. We always have one for medical emergencies; sometimes we even have two. But it's missing. Excuse me." She brushed past him and hurried back down the aisle toward the main cabin.

Kyle wondered if the missing oxygen tank had anything to do with the hijacking. Except if this was a suicide mission, why would they need oxygen? Kyle examined the two IDs in his hand and turned for the cockpit.

Using the phone outside the cockpit, he called Mila to ask her to unlock the door. He passed by the captain's body when he entered the small space. Mila flipped a switch and said something into her headset. Kyle climbed into the blood-stained seat next to her and grabbed the other headset. Mila turned and pulled her headset off her ear closest to Kyle.

"What are you doing?" she asked.

He lifted the driver's licenses for her to see. "I found their IDs. I need to get this info to the investigators on the ground."

"*Now?*"

Kyle pulled on the headset. "Yeah."

"Can't you wait until we're on the ground?" Mila held up her hand. "Sorry, I'm just a bit nervous. Don't want to lose focus."

Kyle didn't want her to lose focus either. "I understand. This won't take long."

She nodded. "Okay, go ahead. But please be quick."

Kyle pressed the switch on the yoke and brought the mouthpiece to his lips. "This is Kyle Adams on Flight 385. I'm a Seattle Homicide detective, and I'd like to be patched through to the FBI with some information regarding the men who hijacked our flight."

"Sure, detective," a female voice crackled through his headset. "We've already been contacted by Agent Weber."

Kyle recognized the name of the special agent in charge of the Seattle field office. Agent Weber was newly appointed, and though Kyle had never met him, he knew Weber had a reputation for getting the job done.

"I'll patch you through to his number."

Kyle listened as a phone began to ring through his headset. Mila remained quiet in the seat next to him.

"Agent Weber," a gruff voice sounded through the headset.

"This is Detective Kyle Adams. I work in the Seattle Homicide Unit. I'm on board Flight 385, and I have some information about our hijackers that I want to share with you."

"Okay, thank you, detective. Go ahead."

Kyle cleared his throat. "I have the driver's licenses from our two hijackers. The first is named Neil Kowalski." Kyle read off the Bellevue address on his license. "The other is Conner Bateman." Kyle recited his address next. He noted the two men were less than a year a part in age. "They both look to be Caucasian," he added.

"Thank you," the agent said. "Is there anything else that might help us?"

"Neither of them had a cell phone on them, which seems strange. I'll look through their bags and let you know if I find anything of interest. But I wanted to let you know their identities first."

"Thank you. We have reason to believe the Somalian sect of the terrorist organization, Al-Shabaab, is behind this attack. Did these men say anything that might confirm that?"

Al-Shabaab? "No. Nothing. They appeared to be nothing more than two middle-aged white guys. Just like nearly half the people on this flight. Including me," Kyle added. *In fact,* he thought, *they blended in so well that if there were more of them on board, it could be anyone.*

Mila was quiet beside him and looked to be trying to familiarize herself with the controls. Kyle decided to keep his thoughts to himself. She had enough to worry about.

"How did you get that information?" Kyle asked.

"An employee of an aircraft cleaning company confessed to planting a gun on your flight after she was threatened by Al-Shabaab terrorists in Somalia."

"These men were definitely not Somalian. And I'm sorry, did you say *a* gun? Because these men had *two* guns. One each."

Mila shot him an uneasy glance as Kyle waited for the FBI agent to respond.

"Affirmative. The employee confessed to planting only one gun on the plane."

"So how did they get the other firearm on board?"

"We're still looking into that. And we'll get to work on this new information you gave us."

The agent's response was less than assuring. They had no clue how the hijackers had gotten a second gun on the flight, which made Kyle all the more apprehensive.

"Feel free to call me back if you find out anything else."

"I will."

The air traffic controller came back on after the call was ended. "Pacific Air 385? Do you read me? This is Oakland Center. Do you read me?"

"I'm here." Mila winced and glanced at her shoulder.

Kyle followed her gaze.

"Mila, I'm going to patch you through now to a pilot who is going to continue to talk you through the descent and landing."

"You're bleeding!" Kyle slipped off his headset. "Were you shot?"

She grimaced. "It's just a graze. I checked it earlier. I'll be fine."

"We need to stop that bleeding. We can't have you passing out before we land. There's a nurse on board. I'll go get her." He climbed out of his seat.

"Fine. But, really, it's not that bad."

Kyle noticed her forehead was perspiring despite the cool temperature of the cockpit. "I'll be right back." He paused when he reached the door. "What if you pass out while I'm gone? How would I get back in?"

"Linda knows the code. I'm not going to pass out. But if I did, she could use the code to open the door. When I don't override it, the door will unlock."

Mila turned back to the controls. Not wanting to distract her anymore, Kyle left the cockpit to find Cora, letting the door close behind him.

CHAPTER SIXTEEN

Kyle assessed the other passengers in the first-class cabin as he walked slowly back to his seat, acutely aware of the 9mm in his holster. Of the seats that remained occupied, there were two men who fit a similar profile to the dead hijackers, at least in their appearance: white and middle-aged. But like he'd told the Seattle FBI agent, so did Kyle, along with almost half of the passengers in the main cabin. *Was it possible one, even two, of them could be in on the plan to take down the plane?*

A third man occupied the seat directly behind Kyle's. He was one of the two men who had carried the bodies to the front. The Black man looked younger than the other two, probably closer to thirty. His hair was short in a military-style cut, and he was dressed more casually than the other men, who looked like business travelers.

The window seat next to Kyle's was still empty, and he spotted Cora still kneeling over the passenger in the aisle in the middle of the plane. Alana was hysterically crying in the seat across the aisle.

"How can this be happening?" she sobbed. "I don't want to die! I don't want to die!"

Linda was bent over her trying to console her. The young woman covered her mouth with her hand.

Alana clutched Linda's arm. "I'm pregnant."

"It's going to be fine." The older flight attendant put her arm over Alana's shoulders. "You just need to take a deep breath and try to stay calm."

Alana covered her face with both her hands as her sobs overtook her words. Kyle moved past them toward the main cabin. He bent over and touched Cora gently on the shoulder when he reached her.

She knelt over an elderly man, and by the color of his skin, it was obvious why Linda had been frantically searching for oxygen earlier. His eyes were closed, and his mouth was open beneath his oxygen mask. His breathing was raspy and labored. A woman in the aisle seat was holding up a bag of IV fluids that was connected to his IV.

Cora looked up at Kyle. Not wanting to alarm any of the passengers further, Kyle leaned closer to her and spoke quietly into her ear. "I need your help," he said. "Up front. Someone was grazed by a bullet."

"Okay. Just give me one minute."

"Thanks."

Cora turned to the passenger sitting in the aisle seat beside her. "Can you keep an eye on his tank's oxygen level? If it gets low, ask the flight attendant to get him another one."

Kyle headed back to first class.

"Does anyone here know CPR?" he heard her ask. "I need someone to keep checking his pulse and breathing while I go up to the front."

When Kyle returned to first class, Alana was still sobbing. Linda tried to pacify her. Kyle stopped next to the empty aisle seat one of the hijackers had been in. An older woman looked up at him from the adjacent window seat. Her white hair was pulled into an elegant bun at the nape of her neck.

Kyle checked the floor before digging through the hijacker's seat pocket.

"What are you looking for?" the woman asked.

"The hijacker's cell phone. Have you seen it?"

Her hand trembled as she felt the three-strand pearls around her neck. "No. Well, actually yes. I remember him on his phone before takeoff."

There was no phone in the seat pocket. Kyle turned and opened the overhead compartment. He pulled out a backpack.

"Is this yours?"

The woman briefly eyed the bag before looking up at Kyle. "No."

Kyle held up the bag for the remaining first-class passengers to see.

"Does this backpack belong to any of you?"

"No," the three men said from the back row of first class. Alana shook her head.

Kyle carefully unzipped the bag. An oxygen mask lay on top of a pile of neatly folded men's clothes. Kyle grabbed the mask and opened the overhead compartment across the aisle and withdrew another backpack.

"Is this bag anyone's?" Kyle turned as he scanned their shaking heads. "No?" He unzipped the bag and rifled through some men's clothing and toiletries. There was no cell phone in either of the bags.

He looked around at the five other passengers in the first-class cabin. "If the hijackers had phones when they boarded the plane, then they have to be here somewhere. There might be a reason they didn't want us to find them. We should all check our bags and make sure they didn't get hidden in one of them."

Kyle grabbed his bag from the overhead compartment and went through his things. One by one, the other passengers followed suit. Kyle glanced behind him as the two middle-aged men looked through their carry-ons. He couldn't see anything out of the ordinary in either of their luggage.

"Did either of the hijackers say anything to you earlier in the flight?" he asked the man seated behind Alana.

The man looked up from his bag. "Me?"

Kyle nodded.

"No. I had my headphones on the whole time."

Kyle assessed his body language for a moment before turning to the man in the row behind him dressed in a suit. "What about you? Did they say anything to you?"

The man shook his head. "No. Nothing." He went back to searching through his bag.

Neither of the men appeared to be hiding anything. Kyle turned to the compartment above his seat. There was one other bag inside. He assumed it must be Cora's, and he reached up and pulled it out.

"I'm ready. Who needs my help?"

He looked up from the bag at the sound of Cora's voice. She had a white first aid kit tucked under her arm. Her eyes fell to the small suitcase in his hands.

"What are you doing?" she asked.

"We can't find the hijackers' cell phones. We know that at least one of them had a phone when they boarded." He set her suitcase on his seat and stepped back to give her room. "Would you mind taking a look to make sure they didn't stick it inside your bag?"

Cora looked around at the other passengers before turning back to Kyle. "Fine." She looked less than happy at the request.

Kyle watched her unzip the bag and look through her things. "It's not here," she said after zipping the suitcase closed. "I thought you needed my help."

"I do." Kyle put up his hands in apology. "I'm sorry, it's just that their phones have to be somewhere." Kyle turned around. "Did anyone find anything?"

A chorus of *no's* resounded from the other passengers.

"That oxygen mask is military-grade."

Kyle turned to the man in the seat behind his, who pointed at the mask in Kyle's hand.

"I'm an Army corporal. Before I got stationed in Hawaii, I did three tours in the Middle East. That mask is the same one our military pilots use."

"It would probably be easy enough to buy one online," the corporal added.

Kyle glanced down at the mask. "Did anyone see either of the hijackers leave the first-class cabin and go to the back?" Kyle hadn't seen either of them get up from their seats, but he'd fallen asleep a couple hours into the flight.

"No," one of the middle-aged business travelers said.

Kyle looked around as the others shook their heads.

"All right, follow me," he said to Cora as he turned for the cockpit, keeping the oxygen mask in hand.

"Who needs my help?"

Kyle took a few more steps before he replied in a lowered voice. "Mila, the flight attendant."

"The pilot?" Cora's eyes widened when he glanced over his shoulder.

"Yeah."

He recognized Mila's voice come over the Intercom as Cora followed him toward the cockpit.

"Ladies and gentlemen, we will soon be making our descent into Honolulu. Please stay in your seats and keep your seatbelts fastened for the remainder of the flight. Thank you."

Kyle was glad to hear that Mila sounded fine, despite her injury. He glanced at the oxygen mask in his hand when they reached the front of the cabin. He turned to Cora.

"Where did Linda find the medical oxygen tank for that passenger?"

"She didn't. We used one of the flight attendants' emergency bottles."

"Hmm." Maybe it had been stashed somewhere by the hijackers. But it was hard to imagine they could've done that without someone noticing. If the cleaner only planted *one* gun like the FBI had said, they still had no idea how the hijackers got the other gun through security. He stepped over one of the hijackers' feet that protruded into the aisle. It also worried him that they couldn't find their phones.

Cora's gaze fell to his hand holding the oxygen mask. "You think the hijackers took it?"

"I'm not sure. Why would they need the mask and oxygen tank?"

She shrugged. "The passengers' emergency oxygen only lasts about ten minutes. But the pilots' oxygen lasts closer to two hours. Maybe it was in case one of them didn't make it into the cockpit?"

He debated this. But if it weren't for him having a gun, which the hijackers weren't anticipating, they would've easily made it into the cockpit. If there were only two of them, even if they were planning to depressurize the plane, they'd both have plenty of air supply from the pilots' oxygen masks. Unless they were planning on keeping one of the passengers alive.

Or there were more than two hijackers on the flight.

CHAPTER SEVENTEEN

Eddie examined the faces seated around his imported rosewood dining table. He was glad to see the Surgeon General, the deputy administrator of NASA, and the chief of space operations for Space Force enjoying their fresh seafood, along with Eddie's board of directors. Their reactions to his latest innovative discovery, however, were much harder to read.

He turned to the large touchscreen on the wall behind him and continued his pitch.

"Through this extensive research, Clarke Pharmaceuticals has not only identified the protein derivative that protects the body from harmful effects of radiation, but we've discovered how to synthesize this protein *without* genetic engineering. The cost-effectiveness and long shelf life of this synthesized protein make it the ideal drug for widespread use in space missions.

"Reducing the harmful effects of radiation to astronauts will have a revolutionary impact on space exploration, colonization, and military operations." Eddie turned to face the government leaders seated at his table. "My company has just begun the process of obtaining FDA approval on this drug. We expect to have it approved in the next six months, and I want to offer this innovative drug exclusively to the U.S. Government before we give that opportunity to our international competitors."

Eddie watched NASA's second in command take a long drink from his wine. While he hadn't expected them to stand up and applaud his groundbreaking announcement, it wouldn't be unwarranted if they did. Eddie looked to the faces of the government leaders, searching for a sign that they were moved by his presentation.

Maybe they weren't understanding the ramifications of this new drug. Eddie cleared his throat.

"Not only will this drug positively impact colonization of both the moon and Mars, but our research has shown it also has the ability to reduce cancers caused by radiation exposure to the Earth's population."

The Surgeon General stared out the large bay windows overlooking the lake as Eddie waited for a show of recognition for what Clarke Pharmaceuticals was offering. But the room was silent.

All heads around the table spun toward the clack of heels on the hardwood floor. Eddie turned toward the door, irate at the interruption.

He'd specifically told the servers not to disturb them for an hour.

"Excuse me, Eddie." It was his assistant, approaching him quickly.

He frowned. She *especially* knew not to disturb him. He held up his hand. "Not now."

She leaned toward him and spoke into his ear. "A plane has been hijacked over the Pacific," she said in a low voice.

"It was headed for Honolulu from Seattle. I think it's Alana's flight."

He snapped forward in his seat. The threatening text hadn't been a hoax.

All eyes from the board members were on him. From their wide-eyed expressions, it appeared they had heard what his assistant had said.

"How long ago did it happen?" he asked.

"The news just broke. I don't think it's been long." She lifted her phone. "The article says they will post updates as soon as they have more information."

"Your girlfriend is on a flight that was *hijacked?*"

Eddie ignored his chief financial officer's question. He never shared his personal affairs with the board. If Alana's flight had been hijacked, it might already be too late to do anything to save her. But he couldn't sit here and not do the only thing that might keep her alive.

Eddie stood from his chair. "Excuse me."

The table was silent as he followed his assistant out of the dining room.

"I need a minute," he told her when she started to follow him to his home office.

"Okay."

He felt her eyes on him as he continued down the hall. He pulled his phone from his pocket and reopened the text he'd received before the meeting. *There's only one way you can save her.* He closed his office door behind him before opening his camera app. He looked into the camera as he lifted the phone in front of his face.

"My name is Eddie Clarke, and I'm the founder of Clarke Pharmaceuticals. I'm guilty of criminal misconduct including fraud and sexually assaulting several of my former employees. I built my company, Clarke Pharmaceuticals, upon lies and false pretenses. For these reasons, I'm stepping down as CEO of Clarke Pharmaceuticals and resigning from the company. More details will follow, as I intend to tell my full story to all major media outlets."

Eddie ended the recording and opened his phone's Internet browser. He searched for news of her flight. A dozen breaking news headlines filled his search results.

Flight from Seattle to Honolulu Hijacked. Airliner Hijacked over the Pacific. Pacific Air Flight 385 has been Hijacked.

Eddie opened one of the articles. It was last updated two minutes ago. His eyes quickly scanned the article.

BREAKING NEWS: It has just been reported that Pacific Air Flight 385, flying from SeaTac to Honolulu, has been hijacked. Radio contact has been made with Oakland Air Route Traffic Control Center, and the flight in still en route. While there have been reported casualties on the flight, it is believed that the crew and passengers have regained control of the aircraft. More updates will be provided as we gather more information.

Reported casualties. If Alana had been a target, that meant she could already be dead. In that case, if he posted that video, he would be risking his life's work and reputation for nothing.

Eddie closed out of the Internet browser and deleted the video he had just recorded. Alana's fate was out of his hands. He knew he should call the police. They might be able to trace the number that was used to send him the photo of Alana on the flight. But it might also launch a very unwelcome investigation into what the text accused him of.

His phone screen lit up with an incoming call from Justin. Eddie lifted the phone to his ear.

"Hey, what'd you find?"

"Not a ton," Justin said. "But the fifteen-digit number you gave me is registered to an Iridium satellite phone or device. I couldn't find any name associated with the number, which seemed odd. But I was able to hack in and access its GPS location. It was over the Pacific Ocean, heading west toward Hawaii. I had only tracked it for a few minutes when I lost the signal. The device might've turned off. Did you get a call or a text from this number?"

"Both, actually. A call and a text with a photo."

"Then it must've been sent through a satellite hotspot, but they can only send images at a very low speed."

That explained the low quality of Alana's photo on the plane.

"Did you hear about that plane that was hijacked?"

Justin must not know about his girlfriend being on the flight. But Eddie wondered how long it would be before the media found out. The less Justin knew, the better.

"It looked like the satellite device could've been in the same flight path. Do you think it could've come from that plane?"

Now he was asking too many questions. "No, it was nothing like that. I just didn't recognize the number. Thanks, Justin."

Eddie hung up before his IT expert could ask any more questions.

Before returning to his meeting, Eddie checked the news again. A new headline topped his search results for Flight 385.

AL-SHABAAB CLAIMS RESPONSIBILTY FOR HIJACKING OF PACIFIC AIR FLIGHT 385

Eddie clicked on the news update. It was only a few sentences.

Leaders of the Somalian sect of the Al-Shabaab jihadist fundamentalist group have already claimed credit for hijacking Pacific Air Flight 385. While U.S. authorities have yet to confirm or deny Al-Shabaab's involvement, a spokesperson for the FBI has acknowledged Al-Shabaab is being investigated as a possible perpetrator of today's events.

He closed out of the article. *Al-Shabaab?* If Alana's flight was hijacked by a jihadist organization, and their motive was terror, then why were they texting him from the flight, demanding that he confess his secrets? *Why are they targeting me?* Or maybe the FBI just didn't have anything better to go on other than the Al-Shabaab claims.

Eddie slipped his phone into the pocket of his dress shirt. His board of directors and three of the country's highest-ranking officials were waiting for him. He couldn't afford not to seal the deal on this new drug. It had taken years of research and cost a fortune to develop.

He opened the door to his home office and pushed his concerns for Alana's well-being, and that of their unborn child, out of his mind. Until he knew otherwise, he would trust that she was okay. And finish closing the biggest deal of Clarke Pharmaceuticals history.

CHAPTER EIGHTEEN

Cora bit her lip as she followed behind the detective. Should she tell him what she'd seen before?

She wondered if anyone else had noticed. Probably not, she decided. Everyone was in shock. There'd been too much going on.

They moved past the first-class galley. Once they were inside the cockpit with the flight attendant, there would be no way to tell the detective. She grabbed his arm and stepped inside the galley.

A look of confusion came over his face when she pulled him toward her. She didn't want any other passengers to overhear. Behind Kyle, Cora watched the man seated behind them step inside the lavatory.

A smile came over the detective's lips. He put his hand on her shoulder. "Look, believe me, I feel it too. But I'm not sure this is the best time for—"

Cora furrowed her brows and took a step back inside the narrow space. "What? No, there's something I need to tell you. Something I saw earlier. What did you think I was doing?"

"Oh." His face flushed with color. "Sorry, I thought—" His eyes searched hers.

She shook her head as a man pushed past them into the small space. Cora recognized him as the well-dressed man seated behind Alana.

The man's eyes scanned the cupboard doors. "Where do you think they keep the alcohol in here?" He slid past Cora and opened one of the metal doors, then slammed it closed when he didn't find what he was looking for.

Cora and Kyle stared at each other in silence.

"I don't know about you two, but I need a stiff drink." He rummaged through one of the lower cabinets.

"What did you want to tell me?" Kyle asked.

Cora's gaze moved to the man as he rifled through another cupboard. "There's gotta be some hard liquor in one of these. I'll even take wine at this point."

She couldn't tell Kyle in front of this man. She didn't want to cause any more panic among the passengers.

The detective glanced at the man behind her and seemed to understand her hesitation. "Why don't we go tend to Mila, and then you can tell me. Unless it can't wait?"

The man stopped going through the cupboards and stared at Cora and Kyle.

"No, it can wait. Let's go." Cora tried to sound casual. They had spiked the man's interest.

She heard another cupboard door open as she stepped out of the galley behind Kyle. They stopped in front of the cockpit door. Kyle turned to her before lifting the phone.

"I'm sorry for what I said earlier, it was stupid of me. "

She heard the lavatory door slam open as she looked at the detective, not sure of what to say. She felt a connection to him too. But there was no time to think about that now. Before she could respond, the man who'd stepped out of the lavatory came up behind them. There was a dark object in the palm he held out toward Kyle.

Kyle turned his attention to what was in his hand. "What is that?"

"It's a satellite hot spot device," the man said. "The military uses these same ones to get internet in remote areas."

Kyle took it from him and examined it closely. The rectangular device was about the same size as a small camera or Garmin GPS.

"I found it in the bathroom garbage. After you guys came up here, the woman next to one of the hijackers remembered him getting up and going to the bathroom about halfway through the flight."

Kyle looked up from the device. "Did you find their phones?"

The younger man shook his head. "Just this."

"So, they used this to get on the Internet during the flight? Why?" Kyle wondered aloud.

The other man shrugged his shoulders. "Maybe they wanted the world to know what they'd done."

Except the FBI agent Kyle had spoken to hadn't said anything about the hijackers uploading any sort of message.

Kyle quickly introduced the Army corporal to Cora. "I'm sorry," Kyle said, "but I didn't catch your name."

"Darnell," the corporal replied.

"*Bingo!*"

They all turned to the sound of the man's voice as he came out of the galley holding an armful of small bottles.

He looked between Cora and Kyle. "I'd offer to share, but some of us better keep their wits about them on this flight."

The businessman headed back to his seat, and the three of them turned back to each other.

Kyle held up the satellite hotspot toward the corporal. "So, we could use this to send photos to the authorities of what the hijackers look like?"

"We could send a small image, yes—if the battery wasn't missing," Darnell took the device from Kyle and turned it over, revealing an empty space in the back. "It was nowhere to be found in the lavatory—I went through all the trash, twice. And I think it's too big for them to have been able to flush it."

"You said you're in the Army, right?"

Darnell nodded. "That's right."

Cora watched a look of suspicion come over the detective's face.

"Where did you say you did your tours in the Middle East?" he asked.

"I didn't. But I did two in Afghanistan and one in Iraq."

"You ever been to Somalia?"

The corporal's eyes narrowed. "No. Why?"

"Was there anyone with you in the bathroom when you found this?"

Darnell scoffed. "No. Why would there be? Is there anything else you want to ask me?" He took a step toward Kyle. "You think I had something to do with this?"

Kyle stared back at Darnell as if waiting for him to answer his own question. Cora noticed the detective's hand rested on his weapon.

"You're welcome for the help in your *investigation*, Detective." Darnell took a step back before he marched toward his seat.

Cora let out the breath she'd been holding in. Kyle reached for the phone beside the cockpit door. Cora put her hand on his arm. She glanced over her shoulder, making sure they were out of anyone's earshot, and leaned toward the detective.

He needed to know what she'd seen—before they went inside the cockpit.

"Earlier," Cora whispered, "when the flight attendant shot the hijacker and saved your life..."

"Yeah?"

"It looked like—up until the last second—she was aiming the gun at *you*, not the hijacker."

His eyes bore into hers, taking in what she'd said. "Are you sure? I mean, we were fighting, moving around quite a bit. It might've been hard to tell exactly what she was aiming at."

"I tried to tell myself that afterward. But I'm sure of what I saw. And there was a moment before she shot the hijacker that you weren't moving. When the guy was trying to strangle you. From where I sat, it looked like she was pointing the gun at you, not him." Cora pressed her lips together and waited for him to respond. She couldn't tell if he believed her.

"Why would she kill one of the hijackers to save me if she was part of the attack?"

"I'm not sure. Maybe she didn't need him anymore. Or she wanted to gain our trust so she could take control of the plane."

He crossed his arms as he looked to be processing what she'd said. "Okay, thanks for telling me. I guess we'll have to keep that in the back of our minds."

Or the front, Cora thought as she lifted the phone. Mila answered after one ring.

"This is Cora," she said. "I'm the nurse."

"I'll unlock the door."

Cora hung up the phone. The plane was surprisingly quiet, aside from a baby fussing in the back. After a moment, there was an audible click as the door unlocked. Kyle made sure no one was behind him before he reached for the handle and pushed the door open.

Cora stepped inside the cockpit, praying the worst had already happened and wasn't yet to come.

CHAPTER NINETEEN

"We're still in the process of gathering information." The Secretary of Homeland Security's bloodshot eyes matched nearly everyone's in the room.

"Save your political answers for the press. Where are we at?" The president looked wearily between the Homeland Security secretary and the FBI director as she waited for a response.

Whitney looked on from her seat against the wall in the Cabinet Room. She'd always admired the president for having no tolerance for political sidestepping.

The president was seated at the mahogany oval-shaped table, flanked by her vice president on her left and the Secretary of State to her right. The other seats were filled with the president's top advisers and several cabinet members who'd been summoned to the emergency midnight meeting.

The Secretary of Homeland Security spoke first. "The flight that's been hijacked is Pacific Air Flight 385 from Seattle to Honolulu. It took off at 3:25 this afternoon with 161 souls on board, including the crew. I spoke with our special agent in charge of the Seattle field office on the way here. He's made contact with Flight 385, and there is an ex-military pilot on board, one of the flight attendants, who is going to land the plane in Honolulu with the help of a 737 pilot talking her through it over the radio."

From her seat against the wall, Whitney watched the president's tense expression. Whitney didn't envy her position. She noted the stark difference in the president's appearance from when she became the first female president four years earlier. The job had certainly taken its toll, and there was no hiding it tonight.

As press secretary, Whitney wouldn't normally attend this kind of closed-door, middle-of-the-night meeting. But she was already at the White House, and this way she wouldn't have to be briefed after the meeting. She thought about some of the other closed-door meetings that had taken place in this room throughout history: The Attack on Pearl Harbor, the Bay of Pigs Invasion, and the days following the September 11 attacks. She never imagined she'd be listening in on one that could go down as another catastrophic event in U.S. history.

"We've dispatched two F-22 Raptors from Hickam Air Force Base in Honolulu to intercept the aircraft. Flight 385 is less than 500 miles northeast of Oahu," the Secretary of Defense added from his seat at the end of the table.

The president let out an audible sigh before the Homeland Security secretary continued.

"There were two hijackers, and each had a gun. They were both seated in first class. They killed the copilot on his way back to the cockpit from the bathroom after he opened the cockpit door. They then killed the captain before he had a chance to secure the cockpit. Two flight attendants were also shot and killed. Fortunately, there was a detective on board who was carrying his firearm, and he killed both hijackers before they could lock themselves inside the cockpit."

"The detective got their driver's licenses off their bodies," the FBI director added. "And our agents in Seattle are headed to both of their homes right now to see what else we can learn. They were both white males in their early forties with no criminal history, but we've got our best analysts looking into them to find out how they're connected to Al-Shabaab."

The president put up her hand. "How did they get the guns on the flight? Do we know?"

The director nodded. "A woman who works for an airline cleaning company confessed to planting a gun on the flight. She showed up at a police station near SeaTac Airport before we knew the flight was under duress. She's originally from Somalia and was sent a video message from Al-Shabaab terrorists yesterday with instructions for hiding the gun on the flight. They murdered her uncle on the video and threatened to kill the rest of her extended family if she didn't comply. They gave her an address to pick up the gun, an abandoned warehouse south of SeaTac airport. We've sent a forensic team to process the building."

"Have we found a connection between these two men from Bellevue and the Somalian sect of Al-Shabaab?" the president asked.

The director shook his head. "Nothing yet."

"How did she get the gun through security?" the vice president asked.

Whitney noticed he looked nearly as run-down as the president.

The Homeland Security secretary cleared his throat. "Many airports only randomly check employees who work on the tarmac, including airplane cleaners."

The president turned to the head of Homeland Security. "But you said the hijackers *each* had a gun."

The secretary shot a sideways glance at the FBI director. "That's correct. We aren't sure how the other gun got on the flight."

"If you don't know how the other gun got on the flight then how do we know there aren't other people involved still on board?" The president looked at both men for an answer.

"Right now, we're looking closely at the crew," the Homeland Security secretary said. "They're the only ones who were able to bypass security before boarding."

The president furrowed her brows. "How?"

"As part of our *Known Crewmember* program, flight crews can bypass TSA screening at sixty airports nationwide. Including SeaTac."

"And how many of the crew are still alive?" The president's mouth was fixed in a frown.

"Two, Madam President," the secretary replied.

"And one of them is now in control of the plane?"

"Like we said earlier, we're still gathering in—" the FBI director's phone buzzed in his suit jacket. "Excuse me." He withdrew the device from his pocket. The room full of top officials watched in silence as the director held up the screen. "It's Seattle FBI," he said.

"Put it on speaker." The president leaned forward in her seat.

The director tapped a button and set the phone on the table in front of him. "This is Director Gibson. What do you have?"

Whitney watched the cabinet members lean in to better hear the male voice that came through the speaker.

"Director, this is Special Agent Weber. We just went to the hijackers' addresses and found both men to be home. We have them in custody. Both are denying having anything to do with the hijacking. They obviously can't be the same men who are on the plane, but we'll fingerprint them when we get back to the station to confirm their identities. They each were able to produce a Washington State driver's license, but they appear to be elaborate fakes. Neither of them know how their IDs were taken."

"Do they appear to match the photos on their driver's licenses?"

"Yes. And they both have a wife and kids who were home when we made the arrests. The men and their families seemed genuinely shocked. But our agents are searching the homes as we speak, seeing if we can find any connections. I'll call you back after we fingerprint them."

"Thank you."

The president adjusted her glasses as the director ended the call. "If both those men turn out to be telling the truth, then who the hell's on that plane?"

CHAPTER TWENTY

"Roger," Mila said through her mouthpiece.

She easily found the two amber *Low Pressure* lights on the overhead panel and flipped the center fuel tank switches to *OFF*. She half listened as the pilot told her what to do next, and she continued to heed his instructions as if she'd never landed a 737 before.

She couldn't believe their plan had gone so wrong. It was her job to check the manifest. But that detective had been added to the flight too late. She'd had no idea there was an armed cop on board. Her eyes drifted to the blood-stained seat next to her. Nearly a year of planning ruined in a few moments.

Mila winced from the pain that ripped through her shoulder when she picked up a black folder from beside her seat. The shoulder of her red Pacific Air uniform was saturated in blood. She groaned and used her right arm to lift the folder onto her lap. It was more than a graze. The bullet had gone completely through her left shoulder, just below the collarbone. At least it wasn't lodged inside her. There were no hospitals where she was going. But it hurt like hell. And she needed to stop the bleeding. She wondered what was taking that nurse so long to come up to the cockpit.

She recognized the FAA standard form for a *Person Carrying Firearm* tucked into the left side of folder. *Seattle Homicide, Detective Kyle Adams. Seat 3B.* He wasn't on the original manifest. His seat was supposed to be empty. She'd been aware that he'd boarded last minute, but she should've been informed that he was armed. She remembered Linda taking a form from the ticket agent who'd escorted the late arrival onto the plane.

It was that bitch's fault in 3E. *Alana Garcia.* If she hadn't been so demanding, Mila would've been the one to accept the paperwork. Her coworker should've given it to her. The pilots and the flight crew always knew if there was someone armed on board. But she'd been so preoccupied with taking care of Eddie Clarke's *girlfriend* that she hadn't seen the paperwork. But what was done was done. Drew and Henry were dead.

A voice crackled through her headset, interrupting her thoughts. "Pacific Air 385, this is Oakland Center. What's your position? We were unable to verify your last position on radar. Can you read off your coordinates again?"

Mila smiled. *That's because I lied.*

She could still abandon their plan. Land the plane safely and be labeled a hero. Save the 154 souls who were still alive aboard the flight. She'd debated when she first came into the cockpit.

Al-Shabaab had been all too eager to take the blame for the hijacking, which should throw any suspicion off herself. Drew and Henry barely had to pay them to force the airplane cleaner to plant the gun on the plane. But forgoing the plan would leave Eddie Clarke unpunished.

"Pacific Air 385, this is Oakland Center. Do you read me?"

Mila closed the black folder and put it back where she'd found it. As soon as that nurse fixed up her shoulder, Mila would carry out their plan. *Where the hell was she?* Mila gritted her teeth as she turned down the volume on the radio and checked their coordinates.

They were nearly 600 miles south of Hawaii. Still about 400 miles from where Spencer was waiting for her. He'd come through so far, but she could only hope Spencer was as good a sailor as he was at making fake IDs. But it would be just the two of them now, sailing to Thailand.

A *ding* came through the overhead speaker. Mila lowered her gaze to the switch that had illuminated. *Finally.* She hesitated before unlocking the door, wondering if it could be possible for the detective to be on to her. But she needed medical attention. If she lost more blood, or the wound got infected, she wouldn't survive the trip to Thailand.

It was too painful to get up from her seat to look through the peep hole in the door. She reached her good arm across and picked up the flight deck receiver.

"This is Cora," a soft female voice came through the phone. "I'm the nurse."

Mila hoped the nurse was alone. "I'll unlock the door."

She turned the switch to UNLOCK to disarm the cockpit door. She heard the door to the flight deck open as soon as she'd hung up the phone.

Mila turned to see not only the nurse who'd been sitting in first class but that hot-shot detective trailing closely behind her. The nurse looked taken aback to see the dead captain in the jump seat. Her eyes lingered on his bullet wound before she knelt beside Mila. She had to adjust the dead pilot's legs to make room for her own.

A look of concern came over her face. "You've lost a lot of blood," she said.

Mila grunted in pain as Cora helped take off her blazer. Out of the corner of her eye, Mila saw the detective start to climb into the captain's seat. *What did he think he was doing?*

Mila drew in a sharp breath as Cora pulled her blouse below her shoulder and pressed a large piece of gauze against her bullet wound.

"Sorry," Cora said. "I'm just applying some pressure to try and stop the bleeding."

"I need to concentrate." Mila shot the detective a look of annoyance. "So, the less people in here, the better."

"I understand," he said. "But I found something that the FBI needs to know about."

Mila's eyes fell to the oxygen mask in his hand. It was meant to be her safety net, along with the medical oxygen tank, in case she didn't make it into the cockpit after they shot the pilots.

He reached for the other headset. Mila eyed the gun she'd used to shoot Henry still tucked beside her seat. The detective was still armed, and she didn't need him wondering why she'd turned the radio volume all the way down. Or giving the authorities any more information.

She turned to the nurse, who lifted the gauze from her shoulder to apply what looked to be some sort of antiseptic to her wound. The cold liquid stung her exposed flesh. Mila grimaced. "How much longer will this take?"

"Not much longer," the nurse said without looking up.

Mila eyed what the nurse was doing. She pressed a clean gauze firmly against Mila's bullet graze while she dug into the medical kit for a bandage. Mila could finish this herself if she had to.

"This is Detective Kyle Adams on Pacific Air Flight 385. I found something, and I need to tell the FBI."

Mila shifted her gaze to the detective. He hadn't wasted any time in jumping on the radio. Now she'd have to come up with an explanation. Fortunately, it hadn't been long since she turned down the volume. It would be easy enough to explain.

"I repeat, this is Detective Kyle Adams on Pacific Air Flight 385. Do you read me?" He turned to Mila. "Is the radio on?"

She decided it would be best to let him tell the FBI about the mask and let the nurse finish tending to her bullet wound, then get them out of the cockpit so she could get back to business.

Mila scanned the controls for the volume to the radio. "Oh, no. I forgot to turn it back up after I took the call from you at the cockpit door." She brought her fingertips to her mouth before adjusting the dial. "There. Now we should hear them."

Kyle repeated himself for the third time into his mouthpiece and explained their lack of radio communication for the last few minutes. Mila winced as the nurse pressed against the exit wound behind her shoulder.

"Sorry," the nurse said. "I need to put pressure on this to try and stop the active bleeding."

"Fine, we'll patch you through in a moment, Detective." Mila recognized the familiar voice coming through the radio from Oakland Center. "But first I need to verify your flight's location. I need to speak to Mila who's piloting the plane."

"I'm here."

"Can you verify your location again? We're unable to pick you up on radar."

Without bothering to look at the IRS display on the overhead panel, Mila gave them another set of bogus coordinates that would put them outside of Honolulu. The irritation in the air traffic controller's voice was obvious when he came over the radio.

"That's *not* where you said you were the last time you gave us coordinates. Unless you're headed back for Seattle."

Mila ignored the detective's inquisitive stare. "Sorry, that was probably my fault. I'm not used to all this. Maybe they got a number wrong, or I accidentally read out the wrong one. I'm a little overwhelmed."

The controller sighed through the radio. "That's all right. At least we know where you are now, and we should be able to detect you on radar shortly. There's a pair of fighter planes out looking for you."

"This is Detective Adams. Can I be patched through to the FBI now?"

"Roger. One moment."

"Don't take too long," Mila warned Kyle. "I need to focus so I don't make any more mistakes."

He nodded. Mila kept an eye on his hands as the FBI came over the radio. He hadn't seemed to notice their coordinates were different from what she said. She doubted he even knew where to look for them. But if he went for his gun, she'd be ready.

CHAPTER TWENTY-ONE

"What have you got for us?"

Kyle looked at the oxygen mask in his hand and thought of the Army corporal who'd recognized it immediately as being military grade. "I found what looks like a military-grade oxygen mask in one of the hijackers' backpacks. We can't find the hijackers' phones, even though a passenger saw one of them on a cell phone at the beginning of the flight. We did, however, find what seems to be a satellite hotspot device in the first-class lavatory, which one of the hijackers used about halfway through the flight. But the battery is now missing from the device. So, one of them might've sent a message or made a call before the attack."

"That could be helpful—thank you. Anything else?"

"One of the flight attendants noticed that the airplane's portable oxygen tank was missing. The one they keep for medical emergencies. And...." Kyle paused. He didn't really think the Army corporal had anything to do with the hijacking. But he wasn't in a position to be too trusting. "There's a guy sitting in first class, seat 4B. He says he's an Army corporal. You might want to check into him. He was alone in the bathroom when he found the hotspot device. He could've used that as an excuse to flush the battery and throw suspicion off himself."

"Oww!" Mila said, flashing a hard look at Cora.

"I need you to turn this way," he heard Cora say.

Kyle looked toward the commotion and watched Mila take off her headset before she turned toward Cora with a pained expression.

"Thank you," the agent said. "I'm afraid we still don't know much. Except that the hijackers' IDs you gave us were stolen. We went to those addresses and found those two men alive and well at their homes with their families. So, we still don't know who those two men were who hijacked your flight. We're still trying to figure out how the second gun got on the plane. There shouldn't be any way they got it through security. Are we alone on the line?"

Kyle glanced to his right. Mila still had her headset off while she impatiently waited for Cora to finish dressing her wound. "Yes."

"Right now, we're looking closely at the crew. They are the only ones on board who didn't go through security."

"Really?"

"Yes. At SeaTac, flight crews can bypass security with their ID badge. And I understand that it's one of the flight attendants who is now piloting the plane. So, until we know more, I wouldn't leave her alone in the cockpit."

Kyle caught Mila reaching for her headset out of the corner of his eye. He had no idea that the crew could bypass security. He thought about what Cora had said to him before they entered the cockpit.

"Thank you, that's all I have," Kyle said. "I think we're ready to get back on with Oakland Center."

"Roger that."

Kyle searched the control panel as they waited to be reconnected with air traffic control, wondering where Mila was reading their coordinates from. They were supposed to be approaching Oahu. But out the windshield, there was nothing but blue ocean for as far as he could see.

He turned to Mila. She was eying him. It looked like Cora had just finished bandaging her shoulder.

He glanced back at Cora. Her head was tilted back, as she stared at the overhead panel. Kyle followed her gaze and found what she was looking at. Their coordinates were lit up in orange under a panel labeled *IRS Display*.

He tried to recall what numbers Mila had given Oakland Center a few minutes ago, but he couldn't remember. But he *was* sure that Mila hadn't looked up when she read off the coordinates. She'd been looking straight ahead.

Cora looked away from the overhead panel and locked her eyes with his. Was she thinking the same thing he was?

CHAPTER TWENTY-TWO

Mila didn't like the way the detective was staring out the windshield. He had to know from being on the radio that air traffic was expecting them to enter radar space very soon. Now that her shoulder had been tended to, she needed them out of the cockpit. They'd be dead long before she made the water landing.

Keeping an eye on the detective's hands, Mila glanced out at the ocean below where Spencer was waiting for her in a sailboat a few hundred miles away. It had been a gift when they found the young radical after it made the news that he was fired from Clarke Pharmaceuticals and convicted for vandalizing Eddie's Maserati after learning that Eddie had slept with his girlfriend. Spencer had pled guilty and got his jail sentence reduced to a few months. And when he got out, Mila, Henry, and Drew were waiting for him. Just like Drew and Henry had been waiting for her following her arrest the previous year.

Spencer was a little crazy, but that was fine. He was reliable, and she wouldn't need him much longer. She'd get rid of him and dump him overboard when they got close to

Thailand. If it weren't for the detective and nurse still in the cockpit, she would've smiled.

She glanced at her blazer on the floor beside her seat that held Drew and Henry's phones in its pockets then turned to the detective who now stared up at the IRS Display.

"You guys better go and let me concentrate on the landing." Mila turned to the nurse behind her seat. "And thank you for fixing up my shoulder."

"No problem," the nurse said.

The detective didn't respond or move from his seat. He still had his headset on. *Why was he still here?* Maybe he didn't trust her. She'd missed a few moments of his conversation with the FBI when she'd taken her headset off.

"Pacific Air 385, can you give us your position again? We are still unable to see you on radar."

The detective pointed to the overhead panel. "Aren't *those* our coordinates?"

Mila shook her head. "No."

"Yes, they are," the nurse said. "See, they're changing as we move."

Mila turned the radio volume all the way down, aware of the detective's eyes on her. If these two weren't going to leave, they left her no choice.

Mila reached her good arm above her head and turned off the bleed air switches. An obnoxious alarm filled the cockpit. She eyed the oxygen mask in her side panel before she slid her hand into the small compartment beside her seat. The detective's hand moved toward his gun as Mila's fingers gripped the pistol.

CHAPTER TWENTY-THREE

All eyes were on Eddie when he returned to the dining room. The chatter around the table immediately ceased as Eddie took his place next to the flatscreen behind his seat at the head of the table. Eddie watched a few of them tuck their phones away. They'd undoubtedly been checking the news on the hijacking, just as he had done.

"We understand if you need to finish this meeting another time," the Surgeon General said, breaking the silence.

Eddie was not about to reschedule. It hadn't been easy to get the Surgeon General, and the leaders of NASA and the Space Force around his dining table. If they rescheduled, it would likely be a remote meeting. And this groundbreaking drug was too important for that.

"That won't be necessary but thank you. It sounds as if things are under control on my girlfriend's flight, and there is nothing I can do to change that. So, I would like to know what your reaction is to this innovative drug we've made and how you wish to utilize it going forward. As I mentioned before, we are looking at a shelf life of up to two years and it will be in the form of an injectable solution."

Eddie observed NASA's second in command and the Space Force chief exchange a wary look.

The chief of the Space Force spoke first. "While this is an impressive development, the timing of it is a little late for us to entertain a contract for widespread use across our space programs. We had a meeting nearly six months ago with another pharmaceutical company that has developed almost exactly the same product. Except theirs has a longer shelf life. They received FDA approval earlier this week." He shot a glance at his NASA counterpart to his left. "And both NASA and the Space Force will be utilizing the drug very soon. Normally I wouldn't give you this much info, but since the FDA just gave it their stamp of approval, there's really nothing to keep secret anymore. The makers behind it will be all over the news in the next week or two."

Eddie glanced at his board of directors, who appeared as shocked as him. If this wasn't such a serious meeting, Eddie would've thought it was a joke.

"What company is this?" There were very few, if any, that could've matched the capabilities of Clarke Pharmaceuticals to develop something like this.

"Regenesis," the Surgeon General said.

"I've never heard of them."

"They're a fairly new company. About two years old."

Two years? How could they possibly have developed a similar product in two years? "Clarke Pharmaceuticals has been laying the groundwork for this research for a decade. Not to mention, spent nearly one hundred million dollars on research and development. I doubt a two-year-old company I've never even heard of could've beaten us to it. Unless they stole it from us."

"That's a strong accusation." The Surgeon General held up his hands. "And it wouldn't seem that they stole it from you when they beat you to it."

It took all of Eddie's willpower to appear calm. He felt heat rush to his face. "This doesn't make any sense. And why haven't we learned of this?" He motioned to his board members seated on one side of the table.

"Well, probably for the same reason that you keep your own research and development confidential," the Surgeon General said. "And why we had to sign non-disclosure agreements before starting this meeting. Regenesis is planning to go public with the drug now that they have approval from the FDA."

Eddie didn't buy for one second that this new company could've developed a similar protein derivative on their own. His research had to have been leaked.

"Who's the founder of this *Regenesis*?" The name tasted bitter as he said it.

"It has two founders," the Surgeon General answered without hesitation. "Henry Voss and Drew Workman."

Eddie felt a knot form in his stomach when he heard the familiar names. *Henry and Drew? They couldn't have.* No company could've beaten Eddie's to the development of this drug. Unless they'd stolen his company's research. Which was exactly what Eddie had done to Henry and Drew when they were working at Elliot Bay University as postdoctoral fellows.

It was Drew and Henry's discovery of a novel immunotherapy that Eddie had claimed as his own and built his fortune on.

The floor seemed to sway beneath Eddie's feet.

"Are you all right?" the Surgeon General asked.

Eddie took a couple of steps forward and collapsed in his chair. He stared across the room at the bay windows overlooking Lake Washington. The sun had set beyond the city skyline on the other side of the lake.

Had Henry and Drew come back to seek revenge against him nearly twenty years later? He doubted they were capable of something like this. They'd been too easy to take advantage of.

Eddie was only vaguely aware of his assistant's heels clacking against the dining room floor as she entered the room.

"I'm sorry to interrupt again."

Eddie turned to the sound of her voice. She'd bent over to speak into his ear.

"Alana's flight has gone missing."

Eddie stared into her eyes. "*Missing?* What do you mean?"

His assistant took a step back, startled by his outburst. She glanced at the others around the table.

"They can't find the plane. From the location the flight gave to Air Traffic Control, they were expecting to pick it up on radar outside of Honolulu. But it's not there. And they're not responding to radio contact."

Ten pairs of wide eyes stared at them from around the table. The Space Force chief's phone buzzed in his pocket, breaking the silence.

"I thought the passengers had regained control of the plane," Eddie said.

His assistant shrugged her shoulders. "I don't think anyone really knows what's happening on that flight now."

A dozen questions swirled in Eddie's mind. Had the plane gone down? Was Alana dead? Had there been more hijackers on board?

The Space Force chief pushed back his chair. "I'm needed on a teleconference briefing with the White House." He stood to his feet, and a few others followed suit. "Eddie, I think I speak for all of us when I say our thoughts and prayers are with everyone on that plane, including your girlfriend."

Eddie nodded, unable to speak.

His assistant stood up straight. "I'll escort everyone out."

Eddie felt some hands on his shoulders and heard a few more condolences as his board and the three state officials left the room. Alone, Eddie stared blankly at the darkening sky out the window.

CHAPTER TWENTY-FOUR

Alana looked at the two empty seats across from her. The detective's worn-out copy of *The Count of Monte Cristo* sat atop his seat. The two of them had been in the cockpit for a while, leaving only five of them in first class. She wondered what the detective was doing up there. Maybe he was telling the authorities on the ground about the oxygen mask and the hijackers' missing phones.

Alana placed her hand instinctively on her belly, as if by doing so she could protect her baby from this horrible situation. Ever since the hijacking started, Alana had been wondering if she was the target. Eddie was one of the richest men in the world.

It was no secret she'd been planning to visit her sister for nearly a year. She'd commented regularly on her sister's social media posts that she couldn't wait to meet her niece. Perhaps that was why Eddie had offered for her to fly private. For security. But it hadn't even occurred to her.

At the time, the idea of crossing the Pacific in a smaller, private jet seemed less safe than traveling on a large commercial airliner. Her eyes rested on the five blanket-covered corpses at the front of their cabin. She was certain she'd never seen the two hijackers before in her life. She hadn't noticed anything suspicious about them while she'd sat behind them for most of the flight. They were average-looking, middle-aged white men. Probably close to Eddie's age.

It was terrifying how well the two men had blended in. She peered at the three men sitting in the row behind her. *Had the cop been asking them questions because he needed their help or was he suspicious of them?* If the men in front of her had been hijackers, it seemed that any of these three men could be too.

It had to be about her. What else could it be? Their attackers hadn't claimed any allegiances to an extremist organization. And how the hell do you get two guns on a commercial airliner?

Alana pulled her phone from her pocket. Still no service. And no damn Wi-Fi on the flight.

There was something about Mila that was bothering her. It seemed strange that she would be working as a flight attendant when she was an experienced pilot.

Oxygen masks dropped from the ceiling above each row.

"What's going on?" Alana heard someone yell from behind her.

Alana threw her phone onto the seat next to her and pulled on her mask.

She turned around. The three men behind her were all in their seats, pulling on their masks. In the main cabin, passengers rushed to their seats. Alana watched a mother put a mask over her little boy, which brought tears to her eyes.

Linda stood in the middle of the main cabin, calling out to passengers to put on their oxygen masks. The flight attendant donned a spare mask from one of the rows before she helped a passenger secure their own. Once the aisle was clear, Linda moved slowly up the cabin, taking a breath from a spare mask that hung from each row as she went.

Alana faced forward. She reached for her seatbelt when she noticed the older woman in front of her struggling to get her mask on. She could see the woman's frail hands above her seat. They were shaking as she tried to pull the strap over her head.

Alana stood up and leaned forward to help the woman secure her mask. The woman patted her hand as if to say thank you before Alana sat down and buckled her seatbelt.

When Linda reached first class, she paused beside Alana's seat to take a few breaths from the spare mask that hung above her row.

"*Why aren't we descending?*" the corporal yelled from the row behind her.

No one had an answer.

Linda moved to the front of the cabin. She pulled on a mask from the first row while she opened the overhead compartment. The first-class passengers watched her withdraw an army-green oxygen bottle. Linda switched her mask to the one attached to the tank and used the shoulder strap to sling the bottle behind her back.

Alana stared out the window at the vast ocean below. Something was terribly wrong. And she wasn't ready to die.

CHAPTER TWENTY-FIVE

"More coffee, ma'am?"

Whitney looked up at the young man holding a carafe. She lifted her empty cup. "Thank you."

She took a sip of the hot liquid as the server left the room. The Homeland Security secretary's phone rang, and all heads turned toward him as he answered. The room went quiet as he listened to the person on the other end of the line.

"For how long?" he asked. "Are they sure?" He lifted his hand to his brow. "Do we have their location?"

The secretary's mouth formed a frown. "How could you lose a plane?"

Whitney bit her lip. This wasn't going to be good news.

"Shit. You need to *find* it. Call me back when they make contact, or you find out where they are." He slammed his phone on the table as the room of officials eagerly awaited his explanation.

"Well?" the president asked impatiently.

"Oakland Center has lost contact with Flight 385."

"For how long?"

"Ten minutes." The Homeland Security secretary sighed. "And they can't verify the plane's last location. The fighter jets weren't able to locate it, and they're heading back to Honolulu before they run out of fuel. Flight 385 should've been within a few hundred miles of Hawaii, but it's not showing up on radar."

The president stared at him in silence, taking in what this could mean. She turned to the FBI director. "What do we know about the two hijackers? Anything?"

The director shook his head. "They both paid for the flight using a prepaid Visa. We're in the process of tracking how they purchased the Visa cards. I'm guessing they used cash, but you never know—we might get lucky.

"And the two men whose IDs were stolen are still being questioned, but they seem to know nothing. Nothing in connection to the hijacking was found at their homes. We did learn that they both belong to the same gym in Bellevue, which is an upscale suburb on the eastside of Seattle. It's open twenty-four hours, and one of our agents confirmed that the gym has had an unusual series of break-ins reported in their men's locker room in the last few months. We believe this is how their IDs were taken and replaced with fakes. There are no security cameras in the locker room, but our agents are going through the footage from other cameras on site.

"We also have agents combing through the airport security footage from this afternoon and using facial recognition software, but we didn't get great footage of the hijackers' faces. They kept their heads down when the cameras were on them, like they knew where they were. I—" His phone rang again. He checked the screen. "It's one of our top analysts," he said before he lifted the phone to his ear. "Director Gibson."

"Put it on speaker, Derek." The president's tone was growing impatient. Whitney didn't blame her.

"Hang on," the director said into the phone. "I'm here with the president. I'm going to put you on speaker." He pressed a button and set his phone on the table, pushing it toward the president.

A female voice came through the director's phone. "Madam President, this is Analyst Skylar Macedo."

Whitney set her coffee cup on the empty seat next to her and leaned forward in her chair.

"I've been looking into the crew on Flight 385 and found an interesting connection between one of the flight attendants and a passenger. Mila Morina, the first-class flight attendant, was previously employed as the corporate pilot for billionaire Eddie Clarke, head of Clarke Pharmaceuticals. She immigrated to America five years ago from Kosovo, where she briefly flew for Kosovo Airlines after serving three years as a helicopter pilot in the Kosovo Security Force. Eddie's girlfriend, Alana Garcia, is on that flight and seated in first class."

"Is this Mila the pilot who is going to land the plane?" the president asked.

The FBI director nodded. "Yes." He turned toward the phone. "We're gonna need more than that, Macedo."

"Hang on, there's more," the analyst fired back. "Two years ago, Mila Morina was fired by Eddie Clarke. She then filed a lawsuit against him for sexual assault. She lost the lawsuit, and Eddie accused her of flying while under the influence of alcohol and drugs. She had begun flying for an associate of Eddie Clarke's and, at Eddie's request, was met by FAA authorities after a landing at Boeing Field in Seattle. The authorities found cocaine in her flight bag, although she denied it was hers. She agreed to a drug and alcohol test, which were both negative. But the FAA still revoked her pilot's license."

The director locked eyes with the president as they took in this information.

"How did she get hired as a flight attendant with a felony record?" the director asked.

"She got her drug charges brought down to a misdemeanor. She was put on probation and ordered to pay a $5,000 fine."

"And," the analyst added, "I don't know if this is relevant, but the heads of NASA and the Space Force attended a private meeting at Eddie Clarke's home this evening."

"So did the Surgeon General." Thomas spoke for the first time during the meeting. The president glanced at her Chief of Staff before turning back to the FBI director's phone.

"I thought this was a terrorist attack?" the president asked. "That video to the cleaner. Wasn't that sent by Al-Shabaab?"

"It looks that way," the analyst said. "But it's possible the hijackers only used Al-Shabaab as a gun for hire. We suspect they may have used the terror organization as a diversion, and that Al-Shabaab was willing to take the blame. We're going through Mila Morina's financials, but we haven't found any large payments going out. Or coming in. She's on a flight attendant's salary, and she doesn't have the means to pay Al-Shabaab very much. But we're still checking into it. We haven't found any contact between Mila and Eddie Clarke. Or his girlfriend."

"Okay, thank you." The director reached for his phone. "Let me know when you find out more."

"Yes, sir."

The president folded her hands as the director ended the call.

"Have we traced that video sent to the cleaner?" she asked.

The Secretary of Homeland Security nodded. "Yes. It was sent from a burner phone, but GPS tracking shows a location in southern Somalia, close to the village where the cleaner is from."

The Secretary of Defense cleared his throat. "I have SEAL Team 2 assembled in Camp Lemonnier. They could be deployed to rescue the villagers in southern Somalia and interrogate the Al-Shabaab terrorists about Flight 385."

The president turned to the Defense secretary. "Do it. Send the team."

He nodded and stood from his seat. "I'll make the call," he said before leaving the room.

Whitney crossed her legs. In light of these events, the scandal surrounding the Secretary of the Treasury that had seemed like such a big deal now didn't even matter. She looked out at the midnight sky beyond the windows lined by amber curtains. Since the call with the FBI analyst, the tone of the room had changed. It was quieter. More somber. The officials around the table seemed to realize that the passengers of Flight 385 could already be dead.

Her phone vibrated in her blouse pocket, interrupting the silence. She'd been ignoring the constant buzzing in her pocket for the last hour. But this was the first time the room had gone quiet enough for it to attract attention. A cabinet member shot her a look of annoyance as Whitney pulled out her phone.

One of the top reporters from the *Washington Chronicle* was calling her. She swiped her finger across the screen to decline. She had over a dozen missed calls and even more text messages from reporters wanting information on the hijacking. Her screen lit up with a new text from a reporter from the *New York Journal*: *Hey Whit, I heard they've lost contact with Flight 385. Is this another Malaysian Airlines situation?*

Whitney silenced her phone and slid it back into her pocket. She was working with her assistant to draft an official statement, but she wanted to have more concrete information before they released it. Right now, they had more questions than answers.

The president turned to the Secretary of Homeland Security. "So, if this isn't a terrorist attack, then what is it? Revenge? Money?"

If the target was Eddie Clarke's girlfriend, Whitney thought, and the motive was money or revenge, then it shouldn't be a suicide mission. But then why couldn't they find the plane?

The director crossed his arms. "Until we have more information, your guess is as good as mine."

The vice president leaned forward in his seat. "Can we monitor Eddie Clarke's bank accounts to see if he's paid some sort of ransom for his girlfriend on the flight?"

The FBI director nodded. "It's likely already being done, but I can make sure."

"So, the woman who's in control of the plane is one of the *hijackers*?" The president seemed to be speaking to no one in particular as she stared at the mahogany table in front of her. "Gibson!" she called after the director, who was heading for the door with his phone in hand.

He turned. "Yes?"

"Send agents to Eddie Clarke's home. We need to know if he was contacted by the hijackers."

"I'm on it. I'll update you once our agents speak with him."

The president's eyes caught Whitney's momentarily as the head of state straightened in her chair. "I just pray we're not too late."

CHAPTER TWENTY-SIX

Kyle couldn't hear anything through his headset over the screeching, repetitive beeping as he waited for a response from Air Traffic Control. He moved his hand toward his firearm and turned to Mila.

"What's that alarm? I can't hear the radio!" he shouted.

The alarm continued to blare from overhead speakers as she stared back at him blankly. He saw the pistol in Mila's hand before he could unholster his own. She swung the weapon toward him. Instinctively, Kyle grasped her wrist and pushed her arm away from him.

The blast from the gun filled the flight deck as a bullet struck the windshield. Kyle expected it to shatter, but the double-paned glass remained intact, despite splintering in every direction.

"Get down!" He could hardly hear his own voice over the ringing in his ears as he yelled at Cora.

Out of the corner of his eye, he saw Cora crouch behind Mila's seat with her hands covering her head. Using both hands, Mila started to aim the gun barrel toward him again. He tightened his grip on Mila's wrist and circled his other hand around her arm, forcing her hand toward the ceiling. The gun went off a second time, sending a bullet into the overhead control panel.

There was a blast from a gunshot inside the cockpit. Alana jumped in her seat. She stared at the cockpit door.

"Someone needs to call into the cockpit and find out what the hell's going on!" the Army corporal shouted.

But no one was risking getting out of their seat to make the call without oxygen. Moments earlier, Linda had returned to the main cabin to help a panicked passenger. Alana craned her neck to scan the rear of the plane, but she couldn't see the flight attendant anywhere. Maybe Linda had already called the cockpit from a phone in the back. *But why hadn't she made an announcement?*

She took a deep breath from the oxygen flowing through her mask. As far as she knew, there were only three people in the cockpit: the cop, the nurse, and Mila. The cop had a gun. But so did Mila at one point.

Another blast came from inside the cockpit. The older woman in front of her let out a wail. The man in the row behind her swore.

Alana gripped her armrest. She feared there was likely only one person still alive in the cockpit. And if that person was a part of the hijacking, they were all as good as dead.

An angry cry erupted from Mila's mouth as Kyle tightened his grip around hers. He wrapped his other hand around her forearm and bent Mila's arm backward. As soon as the gun was pointed at her chest, he slid his finger over the trigger and squeezed.

The shot resonated through the small fuselage. Mila fell back against her seat, blood seeping through the front of her shirt. Her fingers fell away from the gun, and Kyle pulled the weapon from her hand. Her arms fell slack at her sides. Kyle watched the color drain from her face as he kept the pistol aimed at her chest. An audible wheeze escaped Mila's lungs as she struggled to draw in a breath.

Cora got to her knees beside him. She checked Mila's carotid for a pulse, and Kyle realized he was struggling for air. Lights flashed on the control panel, and the alarm continued beeping over the ringing in his ears. He noticed Cora looked nearly as pale as Mila and, for a moment, he worried she might have been struck by a ricochet bullet. She reached across his lap and pulled an oxygen mask out of the panel beside his seat. She put the mask over his head and squeezed the mask under his chin with her fingers. There was an audible hiss as the mask sealed to his face, and he felt a rush of oxygen.

He drew in a deep breath as Cora leaned over Mila and withdrew a mask from her side panel before pulling it on. He recognized Cora's pallor was from the lack of oxygen, not a bullet wound.

"You okay?" He put his hand on her arm.

She nodded after sealing her oxygen mask. Kyle stared at the woman who'd just tried to kill him. She was barely conscious and growing paler by the second.

Despite the small space, they both yelled to hear each other over the oxygen flow and the ringing in their ears, along with the screeching alarm.

"It's the cabin pressure alarm!" Cora yelled. "She must've depressurized the plane!"

"The radio's off!" Kyle said, after taking another deep breath.

He pointed to his headset as Cora turned to face him. "How do we turn the radio on?"

Cora quickly assessed the audio control panel on the center console before adjusting a dial. "I think she changed the frequency. My dad said they always talked to other airliners over the ocean on 1-2-3-4-5," she shouted. "And the volume was all the way down." Cora turned to him as voices came through his headset.

"This is Flight 385!" Kyle yelled beneath his oxygen mask. "We have an emergency. Can you hear me?" He locked eyes with Cora as he waited for a reply.

Cora took Mila's headset off and pulled it on.

"We are only getting background noise when you key your mic," a male voice responded. "If you're wearing the oxygen mask move the little switch on the Intercom panel to *MASK*."

Kyle searched the panels in front of him before he found the silver switch on the bottom of a gray panel. He flipped it up.

"This is Pacific Flight 385! Can you read me?"

"You might need to pull your mask away from your face as you talk."

Kyle squeezed his mask beneath his chin like Cora had. There was a *whoosh* of air escaping from the mask as the seal relaxed from his face.

"This is Pacific Flight 385. We've depressurized! Can you read me now?"

"We read you, Flight 385. We lost your communication. I can barely hear you over the horn. On the right side of the overhead panel is a push button labeled *ALT HORN CUTOUT*."

Cora found the button and pressed it in. The alarm stopped.

"Oakland Center wants you to call them on 6761," the pilot said. "They need to know your position. As soon as you give it to them, get back on this radio and someone will talk you through getting repressurized."

"Roger," Kyle said.

Cora flipped a switch on the middle console before a female voice came through the headset. Kyle's mask resealed around his nose and mouth.

"Pacific Air 385, this is Oakland Center. Do you read me?"

Kyle pulled his mask away from his face. "Yes, this is Flight 385. We have an emergency. There was another hijacker on board. One of the flight attendants. She had control of the plane and has depressurized the aircraft." Kyle turned to look at Mila. He didn't like how close she still was to all the controls. But they'd have to fix one problem at a time. He gripped the gun in his hand and watched her eyelids flutter before they closed. "We need to get the cabin repressurized," he said.

"Roger. Is your VHF-1 radio set on frequency 1-2-3-4-5?"

"Yes," Cora said.

"Good. In a second, I want you to get back on the VHF radio. I'll contact another flight in your proximity and have them talk you through your emergency. If you don't hear from them in the next minute, put out a Mayday to the other flights on 1-2-3-4-5, and someone will help you. But first, can you give me your position? We weren't able to verify the last position you gave us. You're not coming up on radar."

Kyle looked to the overhead panel and found their lit-up orange coordinates.

A different female voice came through their headset. "Flight 385, this is Pacific Air 529. You'll find your coordinates on an IRS display if you look up at your overhead panel."

"It looks like we are N 14345 and W 150493."

There was silence for a moment before the controller responded. "Can you repeat your coordinates?"

Kyle tilted his head back and reread the numbers.

"You said N 14345 and W 150493?"

"That's correct." There was another sharp hiss as Kyle's mask resealed.

The controller swore. "That's almost 700 miles southeast of Honolulu. A long way from where we thought you were. All right, get on your VHF-1 radio and send out a distress call for your depressurization. Call us back if you have any trouble."

Cora flipped the transmit switch on the middle console and turned to Kyle. "The passengers won't have much more oxygen supply," she yelled. She glanced down at the flight attendant. "If she did it, we should be able to flip a switch and repressurize the plane. Unless there's another reason why we lost pressure."

"I think she did it right before she went for the gun."
Kyle lifted the military-grade mask from his lap. "I'm pretty
sure this was part of their plan all along."

Cora scanned the control panel above their heads. "She
reached for something up here. The switch should say
something like 'Bleed Air Supply.' There's just so many
controls."

Kyle climbed out of his seat.

"What are you doing?" Cora asked.

"I want to get her out of the pilot's seat. I don't want
her near the controls. Plus, if we don't get her oxygen, she'll
die. Let me know when the pilot comes on the radio."

"Just keep your mask on," Cora said.

Kyle stepped over the control panel in between the
seats and grabbed Mila by the armpits. Cora moved against
the wall to give him room. He grunted as he tried to keep
Mila's limp body from brushing the control panel between
the seats.

"Take my mask off," he said to Cora.

"I don't—"

"Just for a second, so I can get her near the jump seat."

"Okay." Cora squeezed the mask beneath his chin. "But
hurry."

She watched as he swiftly pulled Mila onto the floor of
the cockpit beside the jump seat. Kyle saw Cora put a hand
over her earpiece. As he retrieved the oxygen mask from
beside the jump seat, he heard Cora unseal her own.

"Yes, that's correct," she said.

Kyle sealed the mask onto Mila's face. He pulled a pair
of handcuffs from his pocket and cuffed her wrists

together. He felt light-headed from the lack of oxygen when Cora tugged on his sleeve.

He climbed back into the captain's seat and pulled on his mask. Cora had taken Mila's spot in the seat next to him. She watched him draw in a large breath, as if making sure he was all right. He pulled the headset back on and Cora went back to searching the control panel.

A male voice came through their headset. "I need you to find the Bleed Air Switches. They should be on the Bleed Air Panel above your head. Let me know when you see them."

Cora mumbled something beneath her oxygen mask. Kyle looked up to follow her gaze.

"It says *BLEED* at the bottom," the pilot added. "Did you find it?"

"Yeah."

"Are they on or off?"

"They're off. But there's a bullet hole in the middle of them," Cora said.

The pilot breathed into the line. "Can you try to turn them each back on?"

Cora pulled on the grab knobs at the end of each switch. "I flipped them both to *ON*."

"Are you feeling a big inflow of air?" the pilot asked.

Kyle and Cora exchanged a look before she responded. "No."

"On the Bleed Air Panel, what does the duct pressure gauge read?"

"Zero."

"It should be reading fifty or sixty if the switches are both on. It sounds like the bullet may have severed the wire to the controls. How long has the alarm been on?"

Cora looked at Kyle before pulling her mask away to talk. "I'm not exactly sure. Five minutes? Maybe a little longer."

Kyle nodded.

"Okay," the pilot said. "If you can't repressurize, then you need to drop to 10,000 feet. I'm going to talk you through a rapid descent."

CHAPTER TWENTY-SEVEN

"On the Mode control panel in front of you, I want you to use the knob labeled *Set Altitude*. Do you see it?" the pilot asked.

Cora's hand found it before Kyle did.

"There's one in front of each of the pilot's seats," the pilot added.

"You do it," Kyle said to her.

She nodded. "We found it."

"Good. Now, select 10,000 feet."

"Done," Cora said.

"Now, press level change. It should be labeled *LVL CHG*."

Cora briefly scanned the control panel before finding the button. "Okay, it's done."

"All right, you should see the throttles come back and feel the nose of the aircraft dip forward as you descend. Is that happening?"

"Yes," Cora said into the headset.

"Your speed should stay the same. So now that the autopilot is set, you'll descend about 3,000 feet per minute. So, you should hit 10,000 feet in about eight minutes. When you hit 14,000 feet, you should be able to breathe normally, but leave the masks on until you reach 10,000, to be safe."

"Okay," Cora said.

"I'm going to check in with Oakland Center while you descend, then I'll be back on to talk you through the landing. Standby."

Kyle turned to Cora after the pilot signed off.

"Thanks for putting my mask on earlier. I had no idea it was in the side panel. I thought the masks would drop like the passengers' do. I might've passed out before I knew what was happening."

She gave him a slight smile, and he felt strangely drawn to her. And not just because of their life-or-death situation. He'd felt the connection earlier, when they made small talk at the beginning of the flight. Even beneath the oxygen mask, it was hard not to notice how beautiful she was.

"No problem, Detective. I couldn't have you passing out on me, now could I?"

Despite the lightness in her tone, he could hear the tremble in her voice. He wondered if she had the same unsettling feeling as he did as the plane sped closer to the water. Toward the inevitable landing they'd have to make without a trained pilot. He wanted to reach for her hand but didn't want to make her uncomfortable.

Kyle picked up Mila's red blazer from the side of her seat. He dug his hand into each of the front pockets and pulled out two iPhones. He turned them on and noticed neither had a personalized photo for a background. The phones were different models, and only one had a fingerprint scanner.

Keeping his mask on, he leaned back and grabbed Mila's limp right hand. He pressed her pointer finger against the sensor. The flight attendant remained unconscious. But from the shallow rise and fall of her chest, he knew she was breathing. A message lit up the middle of the small screen: *Unable to recognize fingerprint.* He held the other phone in front of her face, and a similar message appeared: *Unable to recognize face.*

Kyle turned back around. If Mila had both the other hijackers' phones, hopefully that meant they were the only three on board involved in the hijacking. But there was no way to be sure.

"If there were only three hijackers, then why would they need a military-grade oxygen mask?" He motioned to the jump seat behind them. "One of them could've used the oxygen mask from the jump seat if it's connected to the same air supply as the pilots." With the two jump seats, there would've been enough oxygen supply for four people in the cockpit. Kyle stared down at the mask. Did that mean there were five hijackers on board?

Cora followed his gaze to the gas. "Maybe they brought it as a backup. Or they were planning on keeping one of the passengers alive?"

Kyle thought of billionaire Eddie Clarke's girlfriend in first class. That seemed possible. Maybe Mila had taken the medical oxygen tank and stashed it somewhere on board to use on Alana.

"I'm scared."

Cora's voice tore him from his thoughts. He turned and saw there were tears in her eyes. He reached for her hand, enveloping his fingers around hers. Instead of pulling away, she gripped his hand tight.

"Me too. But we're going to make it, Cora. The worst is over." He squeezed her hand back, knowing his words were to reassure himself just as much as her.

CHAPTER TWENTY-EIGHT

"Here." Kyle extended Mila's gun toward Cora. "Take this. In case she tries anything again."

Cora shook her head. "Oh, I don't—"

"Please. I'm already armed, and it would be a good idea if you are too." He nodded toward Mila. "She's not going anywhere. But use this just in case."

Cora reluctantly accepted the pistol.

"There's already a round chambered, so it's ready to fire. This gun doesn't have a safety, so all you need to do is pull hard on the trigger to use it."

"Okay." She carefully tucked it into the seat pocket beside her.

After checking their altitude, Cora spoke over the radio. "This is Flight 385. We're about to reach 10,000 feet."

"Flight 385, you did good," the pilot said. "You should be able to breathe normally without your oxygen masks. Now the pilot I spoke to earlier, Mila, is she still with you?"

"She was one of the hijackers." Kyle pulled off his oxygen mask. "She's incapacitated."

"Wow. Okay." The pilot's voice remained calm. "Are there any other pilots on board?"

Kyle and Cora exchanged a look.

Kyle spoke first. "No. Mila—the flight attendant—made an announcement earlier and asked if there were any pilots on board. And no one came forward." He turned to Cora. "But you can. You've taken flying lessons, and you've flown this exact airplane *twice* in a simulator, right? And landed it?"

"Well, yes, but I'm not a pilot! That's totally dif—"

The pilot's voice came through their headsets. "I need to do a quick fuel calculation while you two figure out who's going to land the plane. On the center instrument panel, can you read me your total fuel remaining? And can I have your coordinates?"

Cora read off the numbers.

"All right, standby. I need to make sure you have enough fuel to get to Honolulu."

Cora took off her mask and climbed out of the seat.

Kyle lifted one side of his headset. "What are you doing?"

"I want to make sure the other passengers are okay."

He reached for her arm. "Wait. We shouldn't open that door until after we've landed."

"But some of the passengers might not make it until then." She thought of the elderly man she'd helped earlier.

The detective shook his head. "There wouldn't be much you could do for them anyway. And we don't know for sure that there isn't another hijacker on board." His gaze drifted to Mila. "We *think* there were only the three of them, but we can't risk opening that door."

Cora bit her lip as she thought about what he'd said. He was right. But that left only the two of them to land the plane. She couldn't do it. Having a pilot for a dad and taking some flying lessons over a decade ago didn't mean she could land a 737. Even if she'd done it a couple times in a simulator.

"Fine," she said. "But I'm going to make an announcement to see if the other passengers are okay."

Cora stepped over Mila and saw her white blouse was saturated with blood, almost matching the color of her skirt. Cora bent down and felt the side of Mila's neck again for a pulse.

"Her pulse is getting weaker. She needs pressure on that bullet wound."

Kyle shook his head. "That's more than we can do for her. She's in God's hands now."

Cora nodded. "I know, it just doesn't feel right. None of this does."

Cora returned to the copilot's seat. She put her hands on top of her head and stared out the cracked windshield. She squinted from the setting sun that shone almost directly in front of them. There were only a few small clouds between them and the Pacific. Her heart raced. *How could this be happening?*

She didn't want to be responsible for the deaths of everyone on board. Including her own. The thought of her children growing up without either of their parents was almost unbearable.

Cora reached for the Passenger Address microphone at the end of the center panel and lifted the mouthpiece to her lips.

Alana leaned forward to look out her window. It felt as though the plane had leveled out, but her heart was still pounding. The flow of oxygen from her mask had run out a couple of minutes ago. Panicked shouts and cries had filled the cabin. Like everyone else, Alana had worried their descent would continue until they crashed into the Pacific.

They were definitely much closer to the ocean. She pulled her oxygen mask off and turned to see that others around her had done the same. She felt fine, aside from the adrenaline coursing through her.

"We should be low enough to breathe without our masks now," the corporal said, reading the worry on Alana's face.

A female voice came over the cabin PA system. "Passengers, we lost pressure to the cabin, but we've descended to 10,000 feet so that you can breathe without your oxygen mask. Could Linda or a passenger please call the cockpit to let us know you are all right?"

The voice sounded different from Mila's. *It must be the nurse.* She wondered if that meant the cop and flight attendant were both dead.

A scream erupted from the back. Alana turned and leaned her head into the aisle.

Someone cried out from the main cabin. *"Barry!"*

Alana watched a gray-haired woman stand from her seat in the middle of the plane.

"Please," she said. "Somebody help my husband!" Her voice grew more hysterical with each word. "I think—" The woman turned, looking down at the seat beside hers. "I think he's going to die!"

Alana couldn't see the woman's husband aside from his hand that hung into the aisle. The woman brought a hand to her face as a couple passengers rose from their seats to help her. Alana pictured Eddie being notified of her death less than twenty-fours after learning he was going to be father. An image surged to her mind of his knees buckling and him collapsing to the floor.

The news would hit him even harder than this elderly woman in the back. It would crush him.

She pulled her head back to make room for Linda as she rushed through the cabin toward the cockpit.

Cora had barely set down the microphone when Kyle lifted a finger in the air, signaling the pilot had come back on the radio. Cora grabbed the other set and pulled it on.

"Flight 385, this is Pacific Air 781. I've done the fuel calculation," he said. "And I'm afraid you don't have enough fuel to get to Honolulu. You're nearly 700 miles from Oahu. Even if you could return to 35,000 feet, cruising altitude, you still wouldn't have enough fuel to get there. Hilo, Hawaii is about 200 miles closer. I'm going to do another calculation to see if you can make it there. Standby."

"And what if we can't?" Cora asked.

The pilot breathed into the radio. "Then you'll have to land on the water."

Cora slid off her headset. The odds of surviving a water landing in the middle of the Pacific without a trained pilot couldn't be good.

She glanced at the detective, who like her looked lost in thought. If he was thinking the same thing she was, he didn't say it.

The flight deck phone rang, making Cora jump. She leaned over to answer it.

"Hello?"

"Mila? It's Linda. The passengers are terrified. Can you tell us what's going on? Are we going to land soon?"

Cora locked eyes with Kyle, noticing the bright flecks of yellow around his irises. She covered the mouthpiece and whispered to the detective.

"It's Linda. She thinks I'm Mila. Should I tell her the truth?"

He nodded. "Yes. They deserve to know."

Cora took her hand off the mouthpiece. "It's Cora, the nurse. Not Mila. Mila turned out to be one of the hijackers."

Linda drew in a breath through the phone. "*What?*"

"Unless there's a pilot on board who hasn't come forward yet, it looks like I'm going to be the one to try to land the plane. We've been on the radio with Air Traffic Control, as well as another airline pilot flying in our vicinity."

"Oh my—okay. Are you a pilot?"

"No. No, I'm not. But I've taken some flying lessons and landed a 737 a couple times in a simulator."

Kyle gave her a reassuring nod.

Is Mila…dead?" Linda asked.

Cora turned in her seat. "No, but she's shot and unconscious. We—um—have her…contained."

"I'll ask if there's a pilot on board. Although, if there were, I think they would've said something by now. I'll call you back if anyone comes forward."

"Thank you."

"Oh-and I found the medical oxygen tank that was missing. It was stashed in one of the cupboards in the first-class galley."

Mila. "Can you put it on the man in the back—who had the heart attack? His tank might be getting low."

"I'm afraid he's already gone," Linda said.

Cora sighed. It was unrealistic to have expected him to survive the depressurization. "Oh. Okay."

"Mila made an announcement earlier asking if there were any pilots on board," Kyle said when Cora hung up the phone. "But no one came forward."

"I never heard one," Cora said. She'd been preoccupied for so long helping the man who'd had a heart attack. But surely she would've remembered an overhead announcement being made. Thinking of that man, a lump formed in her throat.

"I assumed I just couldn't hear it because I was up here. But I heard Mila make the announcement."

"Did she pick up the passenger address microphone when she made it?"

"I don't know. I was busy moving the captain's body into the jump seat. Maybe she only faked—" Kyle pointed to his headset.

Cora put the other headset over her ears and listened. She recognized the pilot's voice from before.

"I've done a few calculations. You have barely enough fuel to make it to Hilo. They have a large runway, which will help with the landing. I'll do more fuel calculations as you go, since you'll be heading into the wind when you change directions. But you should make it—as long as it doesn't pick up."

Cora prayed they'd have enough fuel to make it to the airport. Landing in the middle of the ocean seemed like suicide.

"I need you to set your autopilot for Hilo International Airport," the pilot added. "Then, we'll go over the landing on your way there. Have you decided who will land the plane?"

The flight deck phone rang, as if on cue.

"We should know in a minute," Kyle said.

"Okay. Do you see the control panel by your right leg that has a small screen on top and a lot of buttons below it?" the pilot asked.

"Roger," Kyle said as Cora pulled off her headset and put the receiver to her ear.

"This is Cora."

"Cora, it's Linda. I made the announcement. But no one came forward. There's no one who's even had a flying lesson on board. People are panicking."

"Thank you, Linda. And tell them to try and keep calm." Cora fought to sound confident. "We have a pilot who's going to talk me through the landing."

"At Honolulu?"

"Um. No. Mila took us too far off course. We should have enough fuel to land at Hilo in less than an hour."

"Sir!" Linda yelled. "Please stay in your seat!"

"Is that the cockpit?" Cora heard a gruff male voice ask in the background. "Who the hell's going to land this thing?"

"Sir!" Linda's voice grew harsher. "Stay back and let me make another announcement!"

There was a muffled sound on the other end of the line. "Linda?" Cora asked.

"Sir, please return to your seat!" she heard Linda yell before she hung up.

Kyle pressed a button on the display screen in between them. Cora felt the plane dip to the right.

"Yes," he said into the radio. "I can feel us turning."

He looked at her expectantly after she put down the phone.

Cora shook her head in defeat. "No pilots on board."

Kyle grabbed her hand and squeezed. "We have you. You can do this. And I'll be right here with you to help."

She felt her lip quiver as she nodded. *What choice did she have?* She'd wondered many times since Wesley died what his final moments were like, and she had a sickening feeling she was about to find out.

Kyle squeezed her hand another time. "Cora will land the plane," he said into his headset.

Cora pulled her headset back on. She tried not to think of all the passengers in the back, especially the children. She closed her eyes and took a deep breath as the pilot spoke calmly over the radio.

"Roger," the pilot said. "Okay, on the instrument panel to the right of the attitude indicator panel is a map display. Do you see it?" the pilot asked.

"Yes," Cora said.

"On the top right you should see *PHTO* displayed and below that a distance should be displayed ending in *NM*, for nautical miles. Can you tell me what that distance says?"

"422."

"Roger that."

If she was grateful for anything in that moment, it was that Kyle was next to her. If only his strength and confidence were enough to get them through this alive.

CHAPTER TWENTY-NINE

Alana sat up straight in her seat, trying to hear what was going on at the front of the plane. A minute ago, she'd heard a woman say there was nothing to be done for the man in the back. His wife's uncontrollable sobs filled the cabin.

By now, everyone around her had taken off their oxygen masks, but the sight of them dangling from the ceiling sent a ripple of fear through her body.

Ever since the flight attendant had made the announcement asking if there were any pilots on board, passengers had been panicking. Everyone had questions. *What happened to the experienced pilot who was flying the plane? Why did they need another pilot?*

In slurred speech, the man behind Alana demanded to know when they were going to land. He'd gone quiet after the oxygen masks dropped, but his voice had returned to a belligerent decibel in the minutes since Linda's announcement.

Linda went rushing through first class toward the cockpit. Alana watched the man sitting behind her follow Linda to the front of the plane, swaying down the aisle from the armful of miniature liquor bottles he'd knocked back after raiding the first-class galley. It left only four of them in first class, and they listened as the drunk man started to argue with Linda.

After a couple minutes, Alana heard Linda yell at the man to return to his seat so she could make an announcement. It was the first time Alana heard panic in the attendant's voice. The Army corporal rose from his seat and marched toward the front. Seconds later, he led the unruly passenger by the arm back to his seat behind Alana's as Linda's voice came over the Intercom.

"Ladies and gentlemen, I need you all to return to your seats and remain calm. I regret to inform you that the flight attendant who was piloting our aircraft was a part of the hijacking."

Alana's stomach turned.

Linda continued. "But there is no cause for panic—she has been um...incapacitated."

Gasps and shouts erupted from the main cabin, making Alana strain to hear the rest of Linda's announcement.

"Please keep calm," Linda continued. "We have someone on board who has landed this exact aircraft in a simulator and has piloting experience. She will be talked through the landing by one of our trained pilots over the radio."

Alana glanced at the two empty seats across from her. Linda must be referring to the nurse. There was an uproar of passengers shouting over each other in the main cabin.

"Heaven help us," the woman in front of her said.

A part of the hijacking. Alana's mind raced. She was sure now that she was the target of the attack. Eddie was worth over one hundred and fifty billion dollars. This had to be about money.

She pulled out her phone and switched it out of airplane mode. But there was still no service.

Linda's voice came back over the Intercom. "I need everyone's cooperation on board to keep calm. In a few moments, I will begin making further announcements to prepare for an emergency landing. In the meantime, please familiarize yourself with the safety instructions on the card in your seat pocket. Thank you."

The first-class cabin went silent. After a few minutes, even the main cabin grew quieter, with less commotion.

Now all they could do is hope and pray that this woman could land the plane without killing them. Tears started to well in her eyes, but she fought them back. Linda was right, they needed to stay calm. For each other. And this wasn't over yet.

Alana looked out the window at the shimmering ocean below. One thing was for sure. If she survived this, she was never flying commercial again.

CHAPTER THIRTY

Kyle stared out the splintered windshield as they listened to the pilot over the radio.

"If we need to," he said, "we'll discuss a water landing. But, at this point, I don't think that'll be necessary. Can you give me your current coordinates and read off the number on the fuel gauge again? I want to double-check my previous calculation."

Kyle noticed the panicked expression that washed over Cora's face when the pilot mentioned a water landing. Although, he couldn't blame her.

Cora read off their coordinates from the IRS Display and their total fuel remaining.

"Thank you," the pilot said. "Standby."

Kyle turned to Cora. She bit her lip and stared at the fuel gauge. She was obviously scared.

"My husband died in a helicopter crash," she said without looking up. "His helicopter crashed while he was volunteering in Samoa last year."

No wonder she was scared. She lifted her eyes to meet his. He noticed for the first time that they were green.

"You know this is different," he said. "We aren't going to die today."

She turned and stared out the windshield.

"The weather is calm. And the pilot is going to talk you through every step of the way. You're already doing great." Kyle cleared his throat. "Do you have kids?"

"Yes."

Her eyes welled with tears, and he realized her children were probably what scared her the most about facing her own death.

She blinked back her tears. "Do you?"

He shook his head. "My job doesn't leave much time for kids."

This was his typical response to this question, but that wasn't *entirely* true. He would have been glad to have kids if his ex-wife hadn't left him. In fact, they were planning on it. Or at least he'd thought they were.

"The truth is," he added, "that I wanted to have children. But since my divorce I've tried to shield myself from getting hurt again. I've had a few superficial relationships—nothing serious. I haven't met anyone who's made me want to take that risk again." He turned toward Cora. "Until today."

She smiled. He felt blood rush to his face. He tried to push away the thought that even if this incredible woman *was* interested in him, they might never have the time to give it a chance.

"You'll see your kids again," he said as a tear slid down her cheek.

Cora prayed what he said would be true. She envied his confidence. She couldn't bear thinking about her children growing up without her now that Wesley was gone. She desperately wanted to hear their voices and tell them how much she loved them. Her phone was still in her purse back in first class. Not that it mattered; there was no cell service. She thought about asking the pilot to pass on a message to them—in case she didn't make it. But that wouldn't be fair to the other passengers. They all undoubtedly had someone they wanted to send their love to as well.

And she owed it to the other passengers not to fall apart. Their lives were in her hands. She forced herself to focus on landing the plane—without allowing panic to take over.

Her hand found Kyle's, and they sat in silence for a moment with their fingers entwined. She liked him too, but she wasn't sure how to say it. It was strange to feel so connected with someone she'd just met. Maybe their connection was only strong because of their situation. But she'd felt it even before the plane was hijacked.

The pilot seemed to be taking a long time on their fuel calculation. She chewed at her lip. She hated being responsible for every life on this plane. She'd had lives in her hands before as a nurse. But that was different: she'd been trained for it.

Cora craned her neck and glanced at Mila lying on the floor behind them. Her chest was still rising and falling. *Why couldn't there have been another pilot on board?*

"We're going to make it," Kyle said, as if reading her thoughts.

His eyes seemed to pierce through hers. She realized she was still holding his hand. She nodded, trying to look more confident than she felt.

"Flight 385, can you read me the distance to PHTO and the total fuel at the bottom of that same display again?"

Cora swallowed and read him off the numbers. *Was there a problem?*

"Thanks. I'm going to check how much fuel you're burning through at this altitude now that you've changed directions. Standby."

"We must not have enough," Cora said to Kyle after a moment of silence on the radio.

"We don't know that yet."

Cora stared out the cracked windshield. The wind howled over the nose of the plane. The sound was much stronger in the cockpit than in the back.

"I lied earlier. When I said I didn't solo in college because I got too busy with nursing school. The truth is that I took the lessons because I felt like my dad wanted me to, but none of them had gone that well. And the thought of being alone thousands of feet above the ground and having to land all by myself freaked me out. So, I quit."

His fingers rubbed against hers.

"Where do you work as a nurse?"

She appreciated his attempt to take her mind off her fears. "I worked as an emergency room nurse for ten years, but I haven't gone back since I had my kids. Wesley's company did really well, and he left me more than I'll ever need for the rest of my life. I've been fortunate to be home with the kids, especially after he died. I miss it though sometimes." She tore her eyes away from the windshield and turned to him. "I bet you've seen some pretty horrible things as a homicide detective."

"I've seen a lot of things, yeah. Some of them I'd like to forget. But I've had some interesting cases, too. I'll tell you about them sometime, over dinner, if you'd like."

She looked into his hazel eyes. "Are you asking me out?"

The sides of his mouth turned upward in a smile. "Yes."

"You mean if we survive this."

"I mean, *when* we survive this."

She smiled at his optimism. "You know, you're the first detective I've ever met. And you're not what I was expecting."

He leaned back in his seat. "What were you expecting?"

"I'm not sure. Someone older, maybe less hair, no sense of humor. Definitely not a charismatic bodybuilder who reads *The Count of Monte Cristo* for fun."

He looked like he was stifling a laugh. "I'm glad I didn't meet your expectations, then."

"Flight 385, this is Flight 871. I'm sorry, but I based my initial calculation on you flying at 35,000 feet, or cruising altitude, and flying into a wind of only five knots. But you're burning through much more fuel at your current altitude. Based on my last calculations, you won't have enough fuel to make it to Hilo. The wind is also coming at you at an increased speed of twenty knots at that lower altitude. You could increase your altitude to 14,000 feet and still have enough oxygen for the passengers, but it still wouldn't cut your fuel consumption enough."

"So, what are we going to do?"

"I'm going to talk you through a water landing. The swell is relatively low, and I'll talk you through it just like I would've for the runway. You'll need to have the remaining crew prepare the passengers for a water landing. I'll give you a few minutes to do that, and then we'll go over the water landing procedure before you start your descent."

"I thought we had enough fuel to make it," Cora said.

"If you were going with the wind and at a slightly higher altitude, you would've been close. But now, this is our best option. It would be exceedingly difficult and dangerous if the engines run out of fuel before you try to ditch. If the engines quit, you won't have the hydraulics to power through the flight controls and you'll lose electricity."

Cora breathed into her mouthpiece. "Okay, I'll let the flight attendant know. How do I call her?"

"There's a black button on your overhead panel labeled *FA CALL*. Press that and then use the phone hanging on the back of your center control stand. After you speak to her, I need you to find the Ditching Checklist in the folder stored in the side pocket of your seat. It's the checklist for a water landing. I'll check back in with you in a few minutes."

Kyle squeezed her hand before she let go to press the flight attendant call button. "At least it's daylight," he said. "I mean, it could be worse."

"Maybe," Cora said. "But just because it's daylight doesn't mean we're going to make it."

He looked disheartened at her lack of confidence. She hadn't meant to sound morbid, but it was hard to stay positive with the odds so stacked against them. She reached for the phone in between them. It chimed a few times before it was picked up.

"This is Linda."

"Linda, it's Cora. We don't have enough fuel to make it to Hilo. The pilot didn't account for our low altitude and increasing headwind when he made the initial calculation. So, we have to land on the water."

The flight attendant sucked in a sharp breath.

"Can you prepare the passengers for a water landing?"

"Linda?"

"Yes, I can do that."

Cora tried not to dwell on the apprehension in Linda's voice. "Do you want me to announce it?"

"Um. Okay, go ahead and tell them. I'll make another announcement as soon as you're done."

After hanging up, Cora held the Intercom in front of her mouth for a moment before pressing the button. She steadied her voice. "Passengers, we have been informed that we do not have enough fuel to make it to the nearest runway. So, we will be landing on the water." She lifted her finger off the button before her voice broke. She took a deep breath and pressed it again. "We have daylight and calm seas on our side. Please prepare for a water landing."

She turned to Kyle after replacing the Intercom. "Do you always look on the bright side?"

"Usually. And especially when there's a beautiful woman beside me."

She shook her head. *If only we weren't about to die.* She tore her eyes from the detective and reached beside her seat. There was a black folder filled with laminated pages. She flipped through them until she found the Ditching Checklist.

"Flight 385, have you found the ditching checklist and made the announcement?"

She held down the switch on the back of the yoke. "Yes, I have."

"Good. And I just spoke with Air Traffic Control, and they've notified the Coast Guard to arrange for your water rescue. Right now, I'm going to have you descend to 1,000 feet while we go through the ditching checklist. Once you reach 1,000 feet, I'll talk you through the water landing. Roger?"

"Roger."

"My name's Jack by the way. Did I hear earlier that your name is Cora?"

"Yes."

"Okay, Cora. Adjust the altitude on the autopilot to 1,000 feet. Then roll the vertical speed thumbwheel up slowly until the indicator says minus 500. Let me know when you've done that, and we'll start going through the ditching checklist."

Cora looked up from the checklist page and stared at the glimmering ocean lurking below the patchy clouds. Throughout the rest of their descent, she would have a full view of the waters that might kill them. She thought of Wesley's final moments and wondered if her husband saw the mountain coming.

She turned her focus from the waters below and set the dial on the autopilot.

CHAPTER THIRTY-ONE

Eddie gripped his phone and paced in front of his living room fireplace. *They'd found the plane. Or at least made radio contact.* He exhaled a sigh of relief. According to the breaking news article, there had been a third hijacker on the plane who'd been taken down after a struggle with one of the passengers.

He was glad he hadn't given in to the hijacker's demands by posting that video. He would've incriminated himself for nothing.

The article also reported that the captain and copilot had both been killed, and it was unclear who on board was going to attempt a landing. It confirmed that there had been a couple other casualties during the hijacking, but the article didn't give any names.

He could only hope Alana was still alive. And that she survived the landing. There was nothing to do now but wait. He moved past the fireplace and looked out the floor-to-ceiling window at his infinity pool, glowing turquoise in the night.

Eddie took a sip from his glass of 1940 Macallan. The taste of the single malt lingered in his mouth after he swallowed. He had purchased the eighty-year-old Scotch at auction earlier that year for over half a million dollars. It was the last available bottle of its kind.

He'd planned to open it when he sold the protein derivative in bulk to NASA, the Space Force, and hospitals nation-wide. But tonight he needed something to take the edge off. Something good.

He clearly remembered the day nearly twenty years ago when Henry and Drew came bursting into the small apartment the three of them shared. They'd barely closed the door behind them when they ecstatically told Eddie about the groundbreaking discovery they'd made in the lab that day.

They'd been abstracting T-cells from mice and modifying them to target specific antigens. Cancer cells. And that day, they'd found that all the mice who'd been given altered T-cells with an antigen receptor specific to the type of cancer the mice had were cancer-free.

More research would need to be done before they announced it and submitted it to journal articles, but their findings were huge. It could've been Nobel Prize-winning research.

Later that evening, Henry received news that his little sister had been killed in a car accident in Wisconsin. The news devastated him. Henry flew east the next morning to be with his family before the funeral, and Drew went with him for support. Eddie dropped them at the airport.

When his two roommates returned home a week later, Eddie had altered their results on their spreadsheet, removing the link between the altered T-cells and the cancer-free mice. Meanwhile, he'd vigorously conducted research of his own in the same university lab. He worked around the clock, confirming and building upon what his roommates had discovered.

By the time Henry and Drew noticed the discrepancy in their results, Eddie had submitted the research to several of the most prestigious medical journals in the world and credited the novel discovery solely to himself. When they realized what Eddie had done, he'd already secured investors in his pharmaceutical company that now led the world in immunotherapy.

They filed a lawsuit, but Eddie had the resources by then to get it dismissed.

Eddie smirked before taking another drink of his Macallan. It had been so easy. Drew and Henry never had what it took to get ahead. They would've never taken those results and run with them the way Eddie had. He had done the world a favor.

Unlike Eddie, Drew and Henry came from money, which Eddie always assumed contributed to their lack of drive. Eddie went without so many things during his childhood that, by the time he was an adult, he knew he'd do whatever it took to never have to go without anything again.

He lifted his phone and reopened an article he'd read earlier that evening about the hijacking. He scrolled through the text, stopping when he found what he was looking for. *While the hijackers' identities are still unknown, Homeland Security has confirmed that they are both Caucasian, male, and appear middle aged.*

There was nothing more in the news about Al-Shabaab's role in the hijacking. Which made Eddie wonder if the authorities had any idea who was behind the attack. He still hadn't contacted the police about the threatening messages he'd received.

He returned his gaze to the pool outside. It couldn't be them. They weren't cunning enough. They were too easy to steal from. And now what was he supposed to believe? That his old roommates conspired to take down an airliner just to ruin Eddie's reputation and have him investigated?

He lifted his glass to his lips. But, somehow, they had managed to steal his company's research and beat him to developing a drug that took Clarke Pharmaceuticals a decade to research and develop, not to mention nearly a hundred million dollars. While Henry and Drew came from wealthy families, they weren't *that* wealthy. Only wealthy enough to make them lack true ambition.

Eddie took a big drink from his glass, letting the Scotch sit in his mouth for a moment before he swallowed. His girlfriend, and his unborn child, were in a life-threatening emergency and his business was turned upside down—all in a matter of a few hours. *Those guys? Bring me down? Make me confess?*

"Excuse me, Eddie."

Eddie swirled around at his assistant's voice on the other side of the room. "I thought you'd gone home. Isn't it—" He checked his watch. "It's after ten."

She pursed her lips. "I wanted to stay in case…."

"In case what?"

"I just wanted to make sure you were okay."

"I'm fine." Eddie waved his hand through the air as if he were swatting an annoying fly. "You can go."

"Okay. But I actually came in to tell you that there are two FBI agents here to see you."

CHAPTER THIRTY-TWO

"Water landing!" the man sitting behind Alana exclaimed. "Too bad Captain Sully isn't here!"

Alana tried to ignore his outburst. Their latest emergency had apparently failed to sober him up.

Linda's voice came over the PA system, drowning out the man's laughter at his own joke. "I need everyone to return to your seats and fasten your seatbelts. As you've just heard, we are preparing for a water landing. Please remove the life vest from under your seat and put it on. *Do not* inflate it until after we have landed. If you require a life preserver for an infant or child under thirty-five pounds, please press your flight attendant call button, and I will bring one to you."

The tremor in Linda's voice only added to Alana's worries as she reached beneath her seat.

"Upon landing," Linda continued, "do not open the rear emergency exits as they will be submerged. Follow the emergency lighting on the floor of the aisle toward the front and over-wing exits only. Check before opening *any* exit to ensure it is not submerged. Rafts will inflate out either side of the front exits. We have an additional three rafts on board, found in the overhead compartments at the front, exit row, and back of the plane. These rafts will self-inflate and should be opened outside of the aircraft."

Alana felt the plane begin to descend.

"Once you have put your life vest on, please take a moment to familiarize yourself with the water landing procedure on the safety card located in the seat pocket in front of you. There will be another announcement when we reach 1,000 feet, at which all passengers should move into the brace position as demonstrated on the safety cards. And I'm going to come around and be asking for a volunteer from the front as well as the back to assist in getting the rafts out of the plane after we land."

"And please...leave all personal belongings behind on the aircraft," Linda added.

Alana pulled her yellow life vest out of the clear plastic bag as the PA system clicked off.

"I think she forgot to mention that those rafts aren't going to matter if we're already all dead," the man behind Alana snorted.

Alana turned in her seat. "Why don't you just shut up and put your life vest on?"

CHAPTER THIRTY-THREE

Whitney sat forward in her chair against the wall of the Cabinet Room as the Homeland Security secretary finished updating the president on the latest turn of events.

"And our agents have just arrived at Eddie Clarke's home. I told our Seattle field office to give me an update as soon as possible," the FBI director added.

"So, who is going to land the plane now?" The president's voice was weary.

"The nurse, who was in the cockpit tending to Mila's bullet wound when Mila attacked the detective. It was fortunate Mila allowed them into the cockpit before she depressurized the cabin. It appears that she was going to run the plane out of fuel as a suicide mission. After killing all the passengers."

"And this nurse is a pilot?"

"Uh, no, Madam President. But her dad is a retired airline pilot. And she's taken some flying lessons and landed a 737 in a simulator."

The president's mouth was slightly agape. Whitney had been to many closed-door meetings with the country's Commander in Chief and, despite the situation, Whitney had never seen the president lose her composure. But tonight was different.

Seeing her dismay, the director added, "There aren't any other pilots on board. She's the closest thing they've got."

The president turned to the Defense secretary on the other end of the table. "And did we deploy fighters now that we've found the plane?"

"Yes, we did that as soon as we found them. They were in a completely different direction and a long way off from where we'd thought. The flight attendant who turned out to be a third hijacker had taken them way off course before the passengers regained control. The fighters should reach Flight 385 in the next twenty minutes."

The Defense secretary's phone vibrated on the table in front of him.

"Take it," the president said.

He reached for the phone. "Secretary Aguilar."

All eyes in the room focused on the secretary as he listened to the other end of the call. Whitney glanced at her empty coffee cup on her lap.

She looked up at the Defense secretary's abrupt voice. "Hang on." He pulled the phone away from his ear and turned to the president. "The fighters are going to be dangerously low on fuel when they reach Flight 385. They're estimated to intercept the airliner in approximately fifteen minutes. The refueling tanker is over thirty minutes behind them. They can put eyes on Flight 385 and confirm its location, but they'll have to immediately turn back to refuel before they catch up again with the flight."

The president shook her head. "Tell the fighters to stay with them as long as they can. I don't want them leaving that plane's side. Have the tanker speed up."

"That may not be possible." The Defense secretary's voice was firm.

"Unless they're gonna go down, I don't want those fighters to leave the plane before it lands."

"I'm not going to risk those fighter pilots' lives. But if they can do that safely, I'll tell them to do it."

"Fine." The president eyed the Defense secretary as he reiterated her request into his phone.

While he was still on the call, the president turned to the FBI director. "Isn't the airliner heading for Honolulu? How far out are they?"

The Defense secretary set his phone on the table and answered for the head of the FBI. "Flight 385 is over 600 miles southwest of Honolulu. They had initially planned to land at Hilo, but they don't have enough fuel to make it there."

Whitney could see lines form on the president's forehead from across the room. "So where are they going to land?"

The Defense secretary pressed his lips together. "It's going to be a water landing."

Murmurs and groans erupted around the table. The president turned to face the FBI director. "So, this nurse who's not a pilot is going to attempt to land the airliner in the middle of the Pacific?"

Before he had time to answer, she added, "What are the odds of them surviving that?"

His expression was tense as he stared back at her, with every face in the Cabinet Room watching him. "It's still daylight, which should help."

The president slammed her palm on the table, rattling the coffee cups and cell phones against the mahogany. Whitney jumped in her seat.

"What are the odds, Derek?!"

The director cleared his throat. "Our experts tell us about sixty-forty." He locked eyes with the president. "Forty that they'll survive."

Whitney heard herself gasp. She watched the president take off her glasses and toss them onto the table before she pressed her thumb and index finger against the bridge of her nose.

"God help them."

CHAPTER THIRTY-FOUR

An oxygen mask covered Mila's mouth and nose, blowing cold air against her face when she awoke. The pain in her stomach was almost unbearable. Her breathing quickened as she stared at the control panel on the ceiling, recalling being shot by the detective before she passed out.

The flight's events were coming back to her. Nothing had gone to plan. Drew and Henry were dead.

She felt resistance when she tried to move her hand toward her abdominal wound. She lifted her head and saw her wrists were bound in handcuffs. Her blouse was soaked in blood. She gritted her teeth.

The nurse and detective were holding hands in the pilots' seats. They spoke calmly as Mila let her head fall back against the floor of the cockpit. They hadn't seemed to notice she was awake.

Mila tried to breathe through the pain. How could they be so calm? They shouldn't have had enough fuel to make it back to Honolulu. Not even to Kona. She tried to slide her wrists out of the metal cuffs but only managed to break a sweat from the pain and her efforts to free herself.

She carefully rested her hands on the side of her torso without a bullet in it and thought about her options. She was *not* going to prison for the rest of her life. She was the *victim* of Eddie Clarke. She'd rather die than serve time for what she'd done as a consequence of his actions. She'd already suffered enough.

Her escape plan was likely no longer an option. Even if they were in the vicinity of where the sailboat was waiting for her, her injuries were too severe to survive the trip. And the detective and nurse weren't wearing oxygen masks, which meant that they had either re-pressurized the plane or dropped below 14,000 feet. And the passengers might still be alive.

She used her elbows to push herself up to a seated position. It took all her willpower not to cry out as the pain ripped through her abdomen. The nurse said something into the radio as Mila studied them. Even if they survived the landing by an untrained pilot, Mila might die before she reached a hospital. And there was no way she could allow Eddie's girlfriend to live. Eddie needed to taste what it was like to suffer a real loss.

She'd take care of the cop first then use his gun to take care of the woman. Mila winced as she pulled her knee to her chest and flexed her foot.

"You picked a good day to land on the water, because the seas are calm."

Cora willed her heart to slow as the plane descended toward the Pacific. She focused on Jack's voice coming through her headset. She would have to treat this water landing just like all the emergencies she'd worked on in the ER and remain inwardly calm despite any external stress.

There was movement out her side window. Cora turned to see a fighter plane flying to their right. An identical plane arrived on the other side of the cockpit. The drone from their own engines and wind howling over the windshield seemed to mask any noise from their accompanying fighters.

"Two fighter jets just arrived on either side of us."

"I'm glad they're with you. They can relay your exact location to the rescue teams once you've landed. Now, the only problem with a calm sea is that it can be hard to differentiate the water from the sky."

Kyle squeezed her hand as the pilot continued. He leaned over to scan the horizon out the side window.

"So, I'm going to talk you through a slow descent—about 100 feet per minute—which we will start after you reach 1,000 feet. With a slow vertical speed, you'll touch down tail first on the water. Then, you'll bring down the nose and skid to a stop."

In her periphery, Cora saw Kyle's head jerk forward in an unnatural movement. She turned toward him and gasped as his hand pulled away from hers.

Mila let out a grunt as she drove her heel into the back of the detective's head. His neck snapped forward from the force of her kick. The nurse jerked her head in Mila's direction, but Mila didn't pay her any attention. She pushed herself up onto her knees—despite the excruciating burn in her torso—and swung her cuffed wrists over the detective's head. The nurse screamed at her to stop as Mila pulled the short chain against the cop's neck.

His head swayed as he tried to pull her hands away with a weak grip.

"Ahhh!" The detective's voice was stifled by the crushing force of his own handcuffs, as Mila pulled with all her strength.

"Stop!" the nurse screamed again.

Cora gripped Mila's forearm with both hands and tried to pry her away from Kyle's neck. Mila leaned back and used her bodyweight to add more pressure on his throat. The detective's movements slowed, and his grip loosened around her hands. The nurse continued pulling against her arm, but she was no match for Mila's strength.

CHAPTER THIRTY-FIVE

Cora was barely aware of Jack's voice over the radio. "Is everything all right?"

There was a crazed look in Mila's eyes. Cora tightened her grip on the flight attendant's arm and tried to release the pressure on Kyle's neck. He appeared to be stunned from the blow to his head. He was hardly putting up a fight.

Mila snarled at Cora. She leaned back, suspending her weight against his neck. Kyle let out a raspy grunt. His gasps for air were becoming barely audible.

"Let go!" Cora screamed.

But Mila pulled tighter. Despite her pallor from her blood loss and gritted teeth, she looked like she was enjoying this. Cora yanked on Mila's arm, but she wasn't strong enough to pull her away from Kyle at this angle.

Kyle's face had turned from red to purple. His eyes were wide, and a large vein bulged from his forehead. His gasps for air had gone silent.

"Cora, do you read me? Do you read me?" There was anxiety coming through the pilot's raised voice.

Cora glanced at the switch to unlock the cockpit door. Maybe she should let the others in to help. She had to do something. She reached for the button, but Kyle put his hand on hers. She turned to him. He was trying to say something. He grabbed Mila's wrist and pulled, but his strength was all but gone.

It looked like he was trying to shake his head. Cora remembered what he'd said earlier about other hijackers possibly being on the plane. Cora watched in horror as his muscular arms fell slack at his sides. His eyes started to close.

Cora grabbed the Intercom and saw the gun Kyle had given her in her side pocket. Mila let out a moan as she pulled against Kyle's neck. Cora dropped the Intercom and gripped the pistol's handle.

She whipped around, locking eyes with Mila's as she aimed the barrel at the flight attendant's head. Mila's eyes widened. Cora pulled the trigger before Mila had a chance to move. The blast resounded in the small confines of the cockpit.

Mila's head whipped backward. Blood sprayed onto Cora's face and her hand holding the gun. The bullet had gone through Mila's forehead above her right eye. Cora's hand was shaking as she dropped the gun back beside her seat.

A male, computerized voice resounded from the radio altimeter over the ringing in Cora's ears. *"Too low—gear! Too low—gear!"*

Kyle had passed out and was leaning to the side. The computerized warning filled the cockpit as it continued to repeat. Cora pulled Mila's lifeless arms forward and lifted her handcuffed wrists over Kyle's head. She pushed his head against his seat and reached across his lap for his oxygen mask. She pulled it over his head and pressed two fingers against his carotid.

Please, let there be a pulse. The seconds felt like hours until she felt a thready pulsation beneath her fingers. She withdrew her hand and grasped him by the shoulders.

"Kyle!" She shook him gently. "Kyle! Can you hear me? Wake up!"

His upper body swayed beneath her hands, but his muscles remained slack and his eyes stayed closed. She stared at his chest until she was sure he was breathing. Then she watched the color start to return to his face.

"Flight 385, can you read me? Please come in!"

Cora could barely hear Jack's question over the gear warning.

"Kyle!"

He didn't respond. Cora knew that his loss of consciousness was likely due to a rise in carbon dioxide from having his airway obstructed. It would take some time for him to regain consciousness.

She heard Jack yelling through the headphones around her neck. "Flight 385! Do you read me? Please respond!"

Cora shot a glance over her shoulder at Mila lying on the floor behind them. Blood oozed from the bullet hole in her forehead. Her eyes were open but stared into nothing.

Cora looked away from the woman she'd killed and turned back toward the controls. Mila was probably only a few years older than herself. Cora never thought she'd be capable of killing someone, but she didn't have time to think about it now.

"Kyle!" Cora shook his arm. "I can't do this without you."

Cora wiped a tear from her face with the back of her shaking hand and pulled the headset over her ears.

"Flight 385! Cora! Do you read me?"

She pressed the switch on her yoke. "This is Cora. I—" her voice broke into a sob. She looked at Kyle—unconscious in the seat beside her—and forced herself to pull it together. She cleared her throat. "There's a gear warning horn going off; I can barely hear you! How do I silence the gear warning?"

"You need to…horn cutout on the…."

Cora searched the control panel in front of her as the alarm drowned out Jack's voice.

"…throttles." She could barely understand his last word.

She looked at the throttles and found a round black button on the right side labeled *HORN CUTOUT*. She pressed the button in. The alarm stopped. In the silence of the cockpit, she became aware of the ringing in her ears from the gun shot.

"Do you read me, Flight 385?"

"I read you. We—we were attacked by the flight attendant who tried to kill the detective earlier. She was wounded and restrained, but she managed to nearly strangle him. He's alive but unconscious."

"And the flight attendant? Are you still under duress?"

Cora looked over her shoulder again. "No. She's dead."

Jack exhaled. "Roger. Are you hurt?"

Cora shook her head. "No." She looked out the windshield, then to her right and left. "The fighters are gone. Why did they leave?" She knew the fighters were only with them to maintain visual contact, but their presence had felt oddly comforting.

"I'm not sure. I'll check with Air Traffic. Have you reached 1,000 feet yet?"

Cora checked the Altitude Indicator Display on her right. "Yes."

"While I check about the fighters, I want you to take a deep breath. Standby."

She turned to Kyle, who looked like he was asleep beside her. She blinked the tears from her eyes. "Please wake up. I can't do this by myself."

"Flight 385, Air Traffic said the fighters had to refuel. They're meeting a refueling tanker that is a little way to the north. They'll come back as soon as they're done."

Even with the pilot on the radio and the planeful of passengers in the back, Cora felt completely alone. The Pacific looked frighteningly close at their low altitude, the ripples on its surface clearly visible. With the fighters gone she could again hear the constant whine of the wind blowing against the cracked windshield.

"We have to start our descent into Maui," Jack said. "So, Australia Air Flight 4422 is going to talk you through the rest of your descent and water landing."

"Oh." She felt strangely attached to the pilot who'd helped her through this far. "I thought you would be the one to talk me through the landing."

"I'm sorry, Cora. But I've run out of time. We have to descend. But you'll be in good hands with Australia Air 4422."

Cora swallowed. "Okay. Thank you, Jack."

"You're most welcome. And God speed, Cora."

Although he meant well, the finality in his sendoff was unsettling. *God speed* sounded like what the passengers of the Titanic were probably told when they realized they were sinking.

"Flight 385, this is Captain Warren on Australia Air Flight 4422."

"Hi Captain Warren. This is Pacific Air Flight 385. Will you be able to stay on with me for a while? I don't want to lose contact in the middle of our water landing."

"Roger, Flight 385. Don't worry, I can stay on the radio for nearly an hour. If you can tolerate my accent."

Cora smiled. "Your accent is great."

"Well thank you, Flight 385. And I like *your* accent also. Now," his tone turned serious, "I'm going to talk you through your descent and water landing."

CHAPTER THIRTY-SIX

Eddie was annoyed to find the two FBI agents had already made themselves comfortable on his living room couch. Apparently, his assistant had taken it upon herself to let them inside. They caught his eyes when he entered the room.

He tried to keep his facial expression neutral. On his walk from the back of the house, he'd been pondering whether to tell them about the threatening text he received before his evening meeting. He shook their hands as the man and woman introduced themselves. They both looked to be in their thirties. The man's suit could have used better tailoring. By the time Eddie took a seat in a velvet chair diagonal of where the agents sat on his couch, he'd decided he would have to tell them.

Maybe they already suspected that he and Alana were the targets of this hijacking. There was no reason to lie. Eddie hadn't done anything wrong. At least not today. And if the text was sent from the phone of one of the hijackers aboard Alana's flight, it would probably be in the hands of the authorities before long anyway.

The male agent folded his hands atop his knees, and Eddie realized he'd already forgotten their names.

"As I'm sure you've heard by now, your girlfriend—Alana Garcia—is on Pacific Air Flight 385 that has been hijacked on its way to Honolulu."

Eddie nodded. "Yes, I have." He realized they might have come to inform him that she'd been killed. He wasn't prepared for that. "Is she still alive? There were reports of some casualties." He looked eagerly between the two agents and tried to brace himself for horrible news.

"We believe she is still alive, yes."

Eddie sagged against his seat with relief.

The agent continued without looking at his partner. "We're here because we found a connection between you and one of the flight attendants on that flight. And, at this point, it appears she was a part of the hijacking."

Eddie's brow furrowed. *Flight attendant?* "I don't know any commercial flight attendants."

The female agent placed a four by six photo on the coffee table in front of him. Eddie's eyes fell to the picture as she spoke.

"Mila Morina."

A knot formed in Eddie's stomach. *Mila?* He was unable to hide the shock that took over his face.

"She worked for you as a corporate pilot on your Gulfstream for over a year. Until she accused you of sexual assault and you fired her. Then, she filed a lawsuit against you. One week later, she was found to be in the possession of illegal substances while piloting a private jet for a friend of yours."

Eddie looked up from the photo and locked eyes with the female agent. She hadn't rattled off all those facts to jog his memory. Her tone was accusatory. They wanted Eddie to know that they knew Mila would have a motive against him.

Eddie wasn't going to allow himself to seem rattled. "He wasn't a friend," he said calmly. But his mind was spinning. *Mila had hijacked Alana's flight, filled with over 100 innocent people, to get back at him?*

He was the one who'd felt assaulted when she refused his advances after making eyes at him for months like she wanted it. When he'd cornered her in the bathroom of his Gulfstream, he thought she'd be ready for him. Instead, she'd insulted him by shoving him against the wall before storming out of the lavatory. She'd even had the audacity to look like a victim. Even though she'd been toying with him. One could hardly blame him for getting angry.

"Are you okay?" the male agent asked.

Eddie gripped his chair's armrest, trying to regain his composure. "Sorry. It's just hard to fathom why she would do such a thing."

"That's partly why we are here," the woman said. "We need to know if you've been contacted by the hijackers on Alana's flight?"

"Um. Yes."

The woman raised her eyebrows. "How long ago? Did you call the police?"

He shook his head. "Earlier. Before there was any news of the plane being hijacked."

The agents both stared at him with cold eyes. Eddie knew they were judging him. But he didn't care.

"It was about three hours after it took off," he added.

"And you haven't told anyone?" the woman asked.

"Well, no. I had no reason to take it seriously at first. And I was holding a very important meeting at my home tonight. The Surgeon General, the Chief of the Space Force, and the second in command of NASA were in attendance."

They didn't look impressed. Quite the opposite. "Was it a text? A phone call?" The woman's mouth was fixed in a frown.

Eddie pulled out his phone. "Both, actually." He opened the message and held his phone out to her.

The man leaned over as the two agents read the message together.

"They took a photo of Alana on the flight. This didn't worry you enough to call the police?" Now it was the man's turn to soundly place blame.

"Like I said, there was no news of a hijacking. I wasn't sure how they got my number, but I didn't think to take it seriously until the news broke over an hour after I received the text."

"But you still didn't call the police?" the woman asked.

"I was in an extremely important meeting until recently."

Eddie didn't care for their suspicious stares. He wasn't the one who hijacked a plane. *He* was the victim here.

The man looked up from Eddie's phone screen. "You said you also received a phone call. Did you answer?"

"Yes. It was a computerized voice telling me to comply with the text message if I wanted to see Alana again. I tried calling the number back, but I got an automated message saying the number couldn't be reached."

"Did you post the video they demanded in the text message?"

"No."

"Okay. I need to forward this message to someone in our tech division to see if they can trace the number," he said.

"Of course." Eddie nodded his approval. Not that they were asking for it. "Go ahead." He refrained from telling them what his IT guy had found. They'd figure it out.

"You got this text at six-thirty p.m. The plane was in the middle of the Pacific. There wouldn't have been any cell service. And Pacific Air doesn't offer Wi-Fi on their flights to Hawaii," the woman said. "Are you sure this photo was taken of Alana *today*?"

"Yes. She was wearing that hat when she left the house. She just got it."

"The message is from a fifteen-digit number." The man looked at his partner. "The hijackers could've sent it using the satellite hot spot that was found on the plane."

The woman leaned forward and looked Eddie in the eyes. "There were also two men involved in the hijacking. They were carrying stolen IDs, so we still aren't sure who they are. According to the passengers, they are both white, and look to be in their mid-forties. Do you have any idea who they are?"

Henry and Drew. But he couldn't be sure. All of today's events felt too crazy to be true. And Eddie didn't want to point out to the FBI why Henry and Drew would hate him after all this time. He didn't need them investigating him for fraud.

"Sorry. I don't."

They didn't look convinced.

"The early reports said you were investigating Al-Shabaab as a likely culprit for the hijacking."

The woman adjusted her blue suit jacket. "They seem to have played a role, but we aren't sure how significant yet. It's possible they were only paid to help get the weapons aboard the flight. And, in light of what you've just shared, it seems they may only be a small piece of the puzzle. They didn't ask you for money, and this feels much more personal than a terror attack."

Because it is personal. They are targeting me through Alana.

"The plane should be landing soon," she added. "We'd like to stay—in case you're contacted again by the hijackers or a co-conspirator."

It seemed in his best interest to appear as helpful as possible. "Sure. How long until they're expected to land in Honolulu?"

The agents exchanged a glance before the woman answered. "They won't be landing in Honolulu."

"Then where?" Eddie asked when she didn't elaborate.

"They're attempting a water landing on the Pacific due to a lack of fuel."

Eddie brought his hand to his forehead. "Who's going to land it? The news says both pilots were killed."

"There's a woman on board with piloting experience who is going to attempt the landing."

Now it was Eddie's turn to raise his eyebrows. "*Attempt?* As in *try* not to kill everyone on board? That sounds nuts. What about Mila? She's a trained pilot!"

The man shook his head. "She was injured when the passengers overtook her."

Eddie stood and turned away from them.

"Where are you going?" the woman asked.

Like it was any of their business. Eddie answered without turning around. "I'm going to need another drink."

CHAPTER THIRTY-SEVEN

Asha looked out the window from the backseat of the FBI SUV as they pulled into the SeaTac Federal Detention Center less than ten minutes south of the police station. The SUV rolled to a stop in front of the towering well-lit facility. The intimidating concrete structure stood nearly a dozen stories tall. Even in the dark, it was obvious that this was no small place, making the severity of her situation sink in.

The FBI agents had asked Asha all the same things the detectives had, plus repeatedly questioned her allegiance to Al-Shabaab. While the detective had told her they'd be lenient, the charges the FBI and federal prosecutor imposed on her seemed quite the opposite. They hadn't appeared to care that she'd acted out of fear for her family. After nearly two hours, they seemed satisfied that she'd told them all she knew.

The two FBI agents had been quiet on the short drive. Asha was grateful not to have to listen to them talk of their everyday lives when hers was ending.

She wondered if Flight 385 had landed by now. She'd asked about the flight before they left the station, but the agents told her that they hadn't heard yet. Asha could only hope no more lives had been lost because of what she'd done.

The agent in the passenger seat turned around. "Normally, people are sent to a jail while they await a trial or sentencing." He pointed out the window. "But due to the nature and severity of your crimes, you'll be held here."

"And," he added, "just because Washington got rid of the death penalty doesn't mean it's off the table for you. When you're charged with a federal crime, such as terrorism, the state limits on the death penalty don't apply."

He allowed his words to sink in as he climbed out of the SUV along with the driver. The driver helped Asha out of the vehicle in her handcuffs and led her toward the building. Asha stared at the entrance to the prison. No one had seemed to care that her relatives were held hostage and going to be killed unless she complied with the terrorists' demands. They also hadn't jumped to her family's rescue like she'd hoped.

The agent who'd spoken to her in the SUV broke the silence as they walked. "You're sure you don't know anything about how a second gun got on that flight?"

Asha's court-appointed attorney had gone home for the night when the agents escorted her out of the police station. Before he left, he warned her not to answer any further questions without him present.

Asha looked the agent in the eyes. "No. I already told you back at the station."

From the way the agent looked back at her, she felt he believed her.

She'd been truly shocked to learn that the hijackers had a second gun on the plane. At the police station, the agents told her the FBI was in the process of interviewing her coworkers. *Had one of them planted the other gun?*

As if reading her mind, the agent added, "Our agents finished interviewing your coworkers this evening. Apparently, Rosalyn was especially disappointed by your actions. I think *betrayed* was the word she used."

Asha swallowed hard. She wasn't going to give him the satisfaction of a response. *Just ignore him,* she told herself. *He's just trying to get you to confess to more.* But she'd already told them everything. She averted the agent's eye contact as she walked.

She still hadn't been able to call Aaden. She had no idea what he was going to say. What if he had heard of her arrest on the news? She could only pray that one day he would forgive her.

When they reached the front entrance, Asha glared at the agent who held the door open as she and the other agent moved through the doorway. All they cared about was the lives of their own citizens. And making sure Asha paid the price for what she'd done.

CHAPTER THIRTY-EIGHT

Cora stared down at the Pacific as the pilot started to talk her through the descent. There was ocean for as far as she could see.

"What's your fuel gauge read?" Warren asked.

Cora tore her eyes away from the vast ocean below and tried not to imagine the plane sinking to the bottom of it. *"2.3."*

"You've got about twenty minutes of fuel. Have you notified the cabin to prepare for a water landing?"

Cora turned up the volume on the radio. The wind was stronger at their low altitude, making it harder to hear the pilot as it whipped against the nose of the plane.

Cora pressed her finger against the switch for the radio. "Yes."

"And you have the ditching checklist?"

"I do."

"I want to make sure you see the note on the checklist that you're not going to lower the landing gear."

"I see it."

"And since you're not putting the landing gear down, there's going to be an alarm—a gear warning horn. You'll have to manually silence it by pulling the circuit breaker, which is on the wall behind the copilot seat."

"A gear warning alarm already went off when we passed about 2500 feet. I silenced it," Cora said.

"That same alarm will go off again after you descend below 1,000 feet since you won't have the landing gear down. You won't be able to silence it at that point. The only way to keep it from going off is to pull the circuit breaker on the panel behind your seat."

"Okay." She did her best to ignore the tremble in her voice.

"According to my weather report, the wind at your location is about ten knots, which means the water should be calm enough that we don't have to worry about landing parallel to any waves or swells. Can you see any white caps or any noticeable swell below?"

Cora sat up straight and examined the turquoise sea out her side window. "Um…no, I can't see any white caps. It looks pretty calm."

"Good. So, before you start to make your final descent here, you need to know that I'm going to talk you through a vertical speed that's slow enough to allow you to land tail-first. I want you to leave the autopilot on until the radio altimeter announces fifty feet. Then you'll turn it off and, at twenty feet, pull back slightly on the yoke. Just an easy pull—not hard—to gently lift the nose just before impact. The tail will hit the water first, then the nose will come down, and you should glide to a stop. After you turn off the autopilot, you'll also have to keep the plane level so you don't dip a wing into the water before you touch down."

Cora bit her lip. She wanted to ask what would happen if she *did* dip a wing into the water. But she imagined it could be disastrous. And worrying about it wouldn't help. "Okay. And how long will the plane stay afloat after we land? We have bullet holes all over in the cockpit and in first class," she added.

"If the aircraft stays intact after the landing, you should have about an hour. Maybe a little less if water comes in through those bullet holes."

If the aircraft stays intact. Cora tried not to dwell on his choice of words.

"Also," Warren said, "I've been informed that a cruise ship is in your vicinity. They've been contacted and will pick you up within a couple hours after you land. The Coast Guard has also dispatched a plane that will reach you before the cruise ship does. The plane will drop off some medical supplies, water, and a few extra rafts. Now go ahead and tell the passengers to brace for impact. Then, pull that circuit breaker for the gear warning horn so it doesn't distract you during the descent. It's labeled *Aural Warn*. Let me know when you're done."

Cora stole a glance at Kyle as she reached for the Intercom. He was still unconscious, but she was glad to see a normal color had returned to his face. She lifted the Passenger Address microphone to her mouth.

Alana turned to the Army corporal sitting in the row behind her. In her periphery, she noticed Linda giving animated instructions to the passengers seated in the emergency exit row at the middle of the plane. "Why did the fighters leave?"

He shrugged his shoulders. "They might've had to refuel. Those Raptors are kept on alert in Honolulu, and they aren't made to fly very long distances without refueling. They probably sent a refueling tanker behind them, but it wouldn't be able to keep up with their speed. My guess is they'll be back as soon as they refu—"

The Corporal's voice was drowned out by the nurse's voice over the cabin Intercom. "Passengers and cabin crew, we will be landing on the water in the next few minutes. Please brace for impact."

Alana turned forward in her seat. She heard a couple people cry out with panic and fear. But within a few seconds, an eerie calm had come over the aircraft. The passengers in the first-class cabin were silent aside from the corporal praying aloud. Alana hoped his prayers would be heard.

"Passengers, remain in your seats in the brace position, as shown in the emergency instructions for a water landing." Alana recognized Linda's voice over the PA. "After we land, the emergency strips will illuminate the aisle toward the emergency exits at the front of the aircraft and over the wings. As a reminder, *do not* inflate your life vests until you are *outside* of the airplane. And *do not* open the rear exit doors as they will be submerged and doing so would result in flooding the aircraft."

Alana heard a sharp *whoosh* from the row behind her. She glanced over her shoulder. Contrary to Linda's announcement, the man behind her had inflated his life preserver, which now puffed straight out around his neck.

As Alana turned back around, she caught the corporal flashing the man a look of annoyance.

They were low enough that Alana could clearly make out the ocean's smooth surface beyond her window. The PA system clicked off and she gripped her armrest as the front of the plane dipped toward the water.

CHAPTER THIRTY-NINE

An image flashed in Cora's mind of the passengers frantically leaning forward in their seats, knowing they could be bracing for death as the plane floated toward the ocean. She replaced the Intercom and pressed the switch on the back of the yoke. "Captain Warren, we've made the announcement."

"Roger that, Flight 385. Before you start the descent, there are a couple more things on the checklist. Ensure that the outflow valve is closed. This is on the pressurization panel above you."

Cora searched the overhead panel.

"Switch the knob to manual," Warren said. "Then move the lever to the left until the needle on the gauge is full left to show *Closed*."

She held the white switch to the closed position until the indicator needle was all the way to the left as he instructed. "Outflow valve closed."

"Then, close the engine and auxiliary power unit bleed valves. These are on the overhead Bleed Air Panel."

Cora glanced at the panel. "The bleed air switches aren't working. We had a bullet go through the overhead panel and it seemed to have severed their connection."

"Oh. Well, just turn them off anyway. If they aren't working, you might have some water seep into the cabin after you land."

Cora flipped the switches. "Okay."

"And one more thing. Upon landing, the engines will likely rip off and you'll lose power. But the radio we're talking on should still work on battery power. So, you can use it to make contact after you've landed."

Cora nodded even though Warren couldn't see her. "Okay."

"And if you lose power, you won't be able to read your coordinates. How about you give me them now, so I can pass them on to the emergency responders."

Cora read him the latitude and longitude from the overhead display.

"Good. I've plotted your position. You're three hundred and forty-five miles from Hilo. Now, let's start your descent. First, set the altitude to zero. Leave the auto throttles on. Then, move the white thumb wheel up slowly to adjust your vertical speed to minus 300."

After setting the altitude, Cora carefully rolled her thumb up the dial, keeping her eyes on the vertical speed reading above it. "I'm moving the thumb wheel. Vertical speed is at minus 300."

"Now, move the flap lever to fifteen and dial the speed back to 170."

"Okay. Done."

"You'll see on the checklist to lower the flaps to forty."

"I see it."

"So, you need to pull the flap lever all the way down."

Cora pulled back on the flap handle next to her seat. "Flaps are at forty."

The subtle ripples on the ocean's surface became more distinct as the plane dropped lower.

"Dial the speed back to—"

A horn blared throughout the cockpit. Cora jumped in her seat, remembering how the captain had warned her about the alarm. She'd forgotten to pull the circuit breaker.

"What's your vertical speed?" Warren asked.

Cora could barely hear what he said.

"How I do I stop the descent?" Cora yelled over the alarm. "I forgot to pull the circuit breaker!"

The pilot said something to Cora over the radio, but she couldn't hear him over the screeching alarm blaring through the cockpit. She scanned the controls in front of her, but she couldn't think over the piercing horn. Cora checked their altitude as she unstrapped herself from her seat. They had passed 800 feet. She only had minutes before they would hit water.

Alana checked her phone one last time. Still no service. She desperately wanted to hear Eddie's voice. Had he been contacted for a ransom? Or had Mila and the two men just wanted to kill everyone on board as some sort of sick terror plot? She had so many questions. And she might die without ever knowing the answers.

She thought of her sister and beautiful baby niece, who she might never see. The woman in front of Alana broke out in sobs. Alana unbuckled her seatbelt. She reached out for the seat in front of her before climbing into it.

The woman looked at her as she sat down. Alana scrambled to put on the seatbelt. After she tightened it, she grabbed the woman's hand. There were tears streaming down her face. Alana gave the woman's hand a gentle squeeze. She looked out the window beside them and saw how frighteningly close they were to the water's surface.

For her entire adult life, Alana had made choices to put her career first. In return, she'd become a wealthy woman and held a powerful corporate position. But now, none of that mattered. All she wanted was a chance to be a mother to her child.

"Brace!" Linda called over the PA system. "Remain seated and keep your heads down! Brace!"

Alana kept hold of the woman's trembling hand and leaned forward, placing her head between her knees. With her other hand, she felt for the toggle that would inflate her life vest, wondering if she'd still be alive when it came time to use it.

Cora checked that the autopilot was still on and slipped off her headset. They were nearing 700 feet as she turned in her seat and got to her knees in search of the circuit breaker on the wall behind her. Her eyes searched frantically for the panel as they soared toward the Pacific.

She found the gray panel above her eye level. The amount of small, black knobs was overwhelming. She skimmed the panel, then forced her eyes to slow down and focus on the small white letters above each breaker. She found the Landing Gear knobs on the right-hand side. There were still nearly a dozen of them. *What was it called again? Gear warn?*

She scanned the small words above the knobs and stopped on the knob at the middle of the panel on the far right: *Aural Warn.* That was it. She pulled the breaker. The horn stopped abruptly, allowing Cora to hear her heart pound against her chest.

The sudden silence was broken by a computerized voice from the radio altimeter. "500."

Cora turned around and strapped herself back into her seat. Warren's voice came over the radio when she pulled her headset back on.

"Flight 385, come in. What's your altitude?"

Cora was unaware of Kyle coming to in his seat beside her as she checked the altimeter reading. "This is Flight 385. I forgot to pull the circuit breaker earlier for the gear warning horn."

"400," the altimeter announced.

"We just passed 400 feet."

"And you've now pulled the circuit breaker?"

"Yes."

"Are your shoulder harnesses and seat belt on?"

Cora swallowed. "Yes."

"Good. You need to slowly roll the vertical speed wheel down until the indicator reads minus 100."

Cora gently rolled her thumb against the wheel. "Okay. It's minus 100."

"All right, when the altimeter announces fifty feet, I want you to turn off the autopilot. You might want to put your hand near it now so you'll be ready. When you go below 100, the altimeter is going to announce every ten feet. I want you to count aloud with it so I know what your exact altitude is."

"300," the altimeter said.

Cora moved her left hand closer to the autopilot disconnect button. "Okay."

"Then, when you get to twenty feet, pull back slightly on the yoke. This should gently lift up the nose right before impact."

Her stomach turned at the word *impact*. The glimmering ocean became terrifyingly close as Cora stared out the cracked windshield.

"200."

"Flight 385, do you read me?"

Cora pressed the switch for the radio. "Yes. Sorry, I read you. We've just passed 200 feet."

"Roger. Start counting aloud with the altimeter after you get to 100. And there's going to be an alarm when you disconnect the autopilot. It's loud, but it will stop after a couple seconds, so I want you to just ignore it."

"Okay."

Beneath them, the soft ripples of the ocean's surface became strikingly clear. She took a deep breath, trying to steady herself. Kyle let out a groan beside her. She turned to see him stirring in his seat, although his eyes remained closed.

"100."

Here we go. "100," she repeated into the radio.

"Roger," the pilot said.

"Ninety."

She said a silent prayer for herself and the passengers.

"Eighty."

She moved her hand next to the autopilot disconnect button.

"Seventy."

An image of her children flashed in her mind.

"Sixty."

She blinked away her tears as they neared the deep blue water.

"Fifty."

"Turn off the autopilot."

Cora flipped the switch as Warren spoke through her headset.

"Auto pilot is off." She could barely hear her own voice through the alarm that sounded.

It startled her, even though the pilot had warned her. She fought to keep her hands steady on the yoke and checked the attitude indicator to make sure they were staying level. The alarm stopped just as Warren had said. Kyle stirred in the seat beside her.

"Forty."

With all the adrenaline running through her, it took all her focus to keep her hands steady.

"Thirty."

This was it. They were practically touching the water.

"Twenty." The yoke dipped to the right in her hands as she repeated the altitude through the radio. A rush of panic filled her chest. If the wing hit before the tail, it might rip off and flip the airplane over. Even if the rest of the plane stayed in one piece, they might all drown before they could get out.

She overcorrected, and the aircraft dipped to the side.

"Gently pull back on the yoke. *Slightly,*" Warren emphasized. Cora eased back on the yoke, but she'd already adjusted it too far to the left.

The nose lifted, momentarily obstructing her view of the ocean.

"Te—" Cora felt resistance on the yoke when the left wing penetrated the water.

The plane angled hard to the side as the left wing violently dragged through the sea before the tail hit the water. Cora gripped tightly to the yoke as her body leaned to the left. Her shoulder strap dug into the side of her neck. Kyle's head smacked against his side window, and she fought to level the plane. The nose slammed forward into the ocean, rocking Cora hard against the constraint of her shoulder harness.

Water crashed over the windshield with such force that Cora was scared it would break. The glass panels creaked from the pressure of the water. The radio went silent at the same time the cockpit went dark. A dim floodlight came on from the ceiling after they lost all power from the controls.

Kyle pulled off his oxygen mask in the seat next to her. Water continued rushing over the windshield as the plane slowed from the water's resistance. She had set the plane down without it flipping over. But it didn't matter. They were going under.

Powerless to do anything else, a scream erupted from her lips. "Noo!"

The lights went out. Alana's head smacked against the seat in front of her as the nose of the plane slammed against the water. Screams erupted from the rear. Water rushed over both sides of the plane, covering the windows with a spray of white.

The older woman beside her let out a shriek. During the initial impact when they'd hit the water at an angle, they had lost their grip on each other's hands. The PA system had cut out in the middle of Linda's commands, and Alana imagined she'd dropped the Intercom. Or worse. Luggage had flown out of the overhead compartments, and Alana thought for sure they were going to tip over. But the aircraft leveled out.

Alana's seatbelt now dug into her stomach from the momentum pulling her forward. A suitcase rolled past her down the aisle. She could hear water continue to pelt against the windows as their speed decreased.

She could only hope their reduction in speed meant they were gliding atop the water and not sinking to the bottom of it.

CHAPTER FORTY

The cockpit plunged deeper into the water and Cora closed her eyes. She felt Kyle's hand on her leg.

"I'm sorry," she whispered.

"You did it."

Cora opened her eyes. They were surrounded by a rush of water as the plane came to an abrupt stop. The sun shone through the thin layer of water that poured down the windshield. It took her a moment to realize they were above the surface. Slowly, the plane leveled out.

She turned to Kyle with her mouth hanging open. "I thought—"

He grinned. "You did it!"

She looked back at the saltwater running down the cracked windshield.

"I thought we were going under." She was unaware of the tears streaming down her face. She turned toward the dim floodlight that had come on above them. The engines must have ripped off during the landing like Warren had said.

"Flight 385, this is Warren. Do you read me? Come in, Flight 385."

Cora pressed the switch on her yoke. "We read you, Warren. This is Flight 385. We've landed. We made it!"

"Roger, Flight 385. That's excellent news. Really good work. I'm going to have you switch to the emergency frequency that your rescue aircrafts are on. It's 1215."

"Roger that. And Captain Warren? Thank you for helping us through that. I couldn't have done it without you."

"It was my pleasure, Flight 385. You did great."

There was a splash outside Kyle's window, then another outside Cora's. Cora turned to her side window to see a gray slide inflated out the side of the aircraft. Cora turned the dial on the VHF 1 radio to the emergency frequency.

"This is Flight 385; we have landed on the Pacific."

A staticky voice crackled through her headset. "Roger, Flight 385. I'm Coast Guard Lieutenant Commander Russo, and we're glad to hear you've landed. I'm piloting a fixed wing aircraft that's headed your way. Are any passengers critically injured?"

Kyle unbuckled his seatbelt and climbed out of his seat. Cora noticed a red welt had already formed on the side of his head where he'd hit the window.

"Linda!" she heard him call after he opened the cockpit door. "How did it go back here?"

Cora could hear shouting coming from the cabin through the open cockpit door. After a few seconds, he turned back to Cora. "Some people are injured, but nothing too serious. Linda thinks everyone survived."

Cora closed her eyes as she pressed the switch on the yoke. "There are injuries, but it seems everyone lived through the landing. No one is critical that we're aware of."

"Roger that. We have your last coordinates, and the Raptors are headed back for you to confirm your exact location. You should see them soon. My plane should be about an hour behind them. You'll have to wait for the cruise ship to pick you up, but we will drop off water and emergency supplies. And three more rafts in case you need them. I'm afraid you're out of range for our helicopters to get to you and back. But we'll send a chopper to the cruise ship when you get closer to shore in case anyone needs immediate medical attention."

"Thank you."

"Happy to help, Flight 385. I'll let you get off the aircraft."

Kyle took Cora's face in his palms when she pulled off her headset. "I know I was unconscious for most of it, but you did amazing. You saved my life—twice." He wiped one of her tears with his thumb, and Cora realized she was crying.

Cora looked into his brown eyes, still in shock that they'd lived. Her eyes fell to his mouth, and she felt a sudden desire to kiss him.

"Now," he pulled his hands from her face. "Let's get off this damn plane."

Cora unbuckled her seatbelt and accepted Kyle's hand when she got to her feet. Cora carefully stepped over Mila's body as Kyle led her out of the dimly-lit cockpit. She said a prayer for the captain as they passed his body in the jump seat.

A red EXIT sign was lit above the cockpit door. Kyle held onto her hand as they moved through the doorway. Cora followed him past the galley.

Aside from the fading daylight coming through the emergency exits, the plane was lit only by the illuminated strips on the aisle floor and the emergency exit signs. The Army corporal stood next to Linda at the front of first class, directing the remaining passengers onto the inflated slides attached to the two front exits. Almost all the overhead bins were open, and there was luggage strewn all over the cabin.

Passengers hurriedly filed off the aircraft. Some were crying, others were clutching their children, and some looked to be in shock. Cora pressed her hand against the wall for support as the plane rocked beneath her feet.

She looked out the exit to her left and saw the slide was already full of passengers. The Corporal held out his arm when a passenger moved toward the exit.

"That side's full." He motioned to the opposite door. "Go out this way."

Cora watched the woman hurry out the other exit, noticing a gash on her cheek and how she cradled her arm when she moved. Somehow, she felt responsible for the woman's injuries and prayed there weren't other passengers worse off.

From the angle of the floor, Cora knew the tail must be submerged. She looked beyond the passengers shuffling toward the front of the plane and was glad to see the plane looked to be intact. A few of the passengers eyed Cora and Kyle as they deplaned, but they were too focused on getting off the aircraft to pay them much attention.

Linda followed one of the passenger's gaze and turned around. She smiled when her eyes met Cora's. She squeezed her gently on the shoulder. "I knew you could do it," she said.

"Thank you."

Linda held up her hand to signal one of the passengers to wait. "You two can go."

Cora shook her head. "I'll wait until everyone is off."

Kyle kept hold of her hand. "I'll wait too."

Linda nodded and motioned for the passenger at the front of the line to get off.

She turned to the corporal. "I don't want these slides getting too full. Only let four more people on."

He nodded and directed the next passenger toward the exit.

She cupped her hands around her mouth and spoke toward the back of the plane. "We can only fit four more people in this slide! After that, I need everyone to disembark using the over-wing exits in the middle of the plane."

The passengers at the back of first class turned and waited in line for the middle exits, which passengers were already leaving through. Linda explained to the passengers in the front rafts that they could stay attached to the aircraft as long as it stayed afloat.

"If the plane sinks before we are rescued, there is a seatbelt cutter in the front flap of the slide to cut the ties."

After Linda finished addressing the passengers, she turned to Kyle and Cora. "You two need to grab your life vests from under your seats before you get off."

Linda moved toward the rear of the plane, leaving the corporal to finish directing the last few passengers onto the inflated slide. Cora followed after the flight attendant, stopping to pull her life vest out from underneath her seat. She pulled it over her head and moved to the back of line near the partition to first class. She turned to make sure Kyle was with her and watched the Corporal put his hand on Kyle's shoulder.

"You want to help me carry these bodies out after everyone gets off?" he asked.

"Yeah," Kyle said. "Let's go get the captain out of the cockpit."

The corporal followed Kyle to the front of the plane. Cora turned back around. She stepped over a suitcase and moved with the line. When she moved into the main cabin, she saw that several rows of seats had come loose from the floor and had fallen into the aisle. Suitcases, backpacks, and clothing were everywhere. The line moved slowly as wounded passengers stepped over the debris to exit one-by-one.

When Cora neared the exit doors, she saw Barry—now dead—in his seat a few rows behind the exit row. His wife stayed in her seat beside him, making no effort to get up.

There were still nearly a dozen people in line coming from the back when the man assisting at the exit waved Cora forward. Linda had stepped out onto the wing and held her hand out to Cora.

"Ma'am," Cora said to the woman beside Barry. "Aren't you coming?"

Barry's wife looked up at Cora, grief-stricken. She shook her head. "Not without my husband."

"Hurry up!" a bearded man called out from the back of the line.

Cora held the woman's gaze as she paused in the opening. "There are two men at the front who will help. They can get your husband. You should come now."

"I'll wait."

Cora accepted Linda's hand and climbed onto the wing. A couple inches of water covered her feet. There were two life rafts tied to the wing. One was already packed with people and the other was nearly as full. The sun had sunk below the horizon. Cora realized it would be dark long before they were rescued by the cruise ship. Linda directed her toward the closer raft, and Cora stepped carefully across the slippery surface to avoid a fall.

Passengers crammed together to make room for Cora when she reached the raft. A man offered his hand to help stabilize her when she climbed in. She looked up at the sound of jet engines and saw lights from the two fighters. People around her waved and hollered as the Raptors soared above them in the twilight sky.

Cora squeezed closer to the man next to her to make room for a woman to climb into the raft. She kept her eyes on the emergency exit, watching for Kyle. Her raft was nearing capacity, and she realized he would probably end up in the one on the opposite wing. She knew he'd be getting off last since he was helping to carry out the deceased. But, selfishly, she wanted him beside her.

Kyle stepped over an open suitcase, careful not to lose hold of the captain's armpits as he and Darnell carried his body down the aisle. It had grown darker inside the plane since they landed. When they reached the main cabin, Kyle felt a cold sensation in his feet. He looked down to see he was standing in a puddle of water, which he guessed was coming in from one of the bullet holes. The plane had started to dip to the side.

They continued toward the wing exits, where fewer than a dozen people were still waiting to get off. He slowed his pace as the corporal maneuvered over a row of seats on their sides.

"I'm sorry for being suspicious of you earlier," Kyle said.

Darnell met his gaze.

"I just didn't know who to trust," Kyle added.

"It's all right," Darnell said. "I—

"Hey, there's water on the floor!" a man shouted from the back. "This thing is *sinking*! Hurry up!"

Elderly passengers were climbing out of each of the wing exits. Kyle craned his neck to see the man who was yelling was at the back of line behind the exits. Kyle started to climb over the detached seats when a woman cried out.

Darnell and Kyle turned to see a woman pulling herself up in a row of seats next to a man with a dark beard in the back.

"Don't push me!" she screamed at him.

"Hey!" Darnell called out, still holding on to the captain's legs. "There's no need to get violent! Everyone's going to get off."

The elderly passengers stood frozen in the exit doors as they watched the commotion. Kyle and Darnell took a few more steps as the bearded man crouched down and peered through the windows.

"The rafts are full!" Panic was evident in the man's voice. "I'm not gonna float in the water all night with the sharks!"

A loud creak escaped from the belly of the aircraft before it tilted farther to the side. Kyle fell against the seat next him.

"Screw you all!" the man shouted and turned for the rear of the plane.

Darnell turned around. "Hey! What are you doing?"

The man ignored him and disappeared behind the rear lavatory. Kyle heard a faint *hiss* before the floor shifted beneath his feet. The back of the plane dropped, knocking Darnell off balance. Kyle was thrown forward as Darnell lost his grip on the captain's legs. Kyle let go of the captain and grabbed on to a seat as water rushed toward them from the rear.

CHAPTER FORTY-ONE

Cora turned toward a *pop* at the rear of the plane. Unsure of what caused the sound, her eyes scanned the tail of the aircraft until she saw movement at the rear exit. Only the top of the door was above water, and Cora watched in horror alongside the other passengers as the door opened and water began to immediately rush in.

An elderly woman fell out of the over-wing exit, and Linda helped her to her feet as another passenger jumped out the opening. The tail sank deeper into the water, and the plane tilted in their direction. Water engulfed the top of the wing, causing Linda and the two passengers to fall into the water.

The raft's mooring line was pulled taut by the submerged wing. A woman next to Cora cried out as water came over the side of the raft.

"Cut the rope!" Cora told the man beside her.

He reached for the knife attached to the mooring line near the raft. More water flooded into the raft as the man hastily severed the tie. A man jumped from the over-wing exit, and Cora was disappointed to see it wasn't Kyle.

Linda and the three passengers swam with frantic strokes toward Cora's drifting raft, their water-activated lights flickering on the shoulders of their life vests. The people on the other side of Cora's raft grabbed hold of the evacuation slide attached to the front exit to stop them from drifting away.

Cora held out her arms for Linda when she neared the raft. With the help of the man beside her, they pulled Linda aboard, followed by the three passengers. It was nearly dark, but through the plane's exit doors, Cora could see another raft also cut away from the opposite wing. They now drifted away from the plane.

Aside from the vertical stabilizer, the tail of the plane was completely underwater.

A woman yelled out from the inflated slide attached the front exit. "We need to break away from the plane!"

It sounded like Alana Garcia.

"No, you don't!" Linda responded from beside Cora. "The ties on that raft are made to break when any tension is pulled. Before the plane sinks, those ties will detach."

Cora looked back at the plane. *It's already sinking,* she thought. It was too dark to see inside. She stared at the over-wing exit, where water was starting to flow into the plane. *Where was Kyle? Why wasn't he coming out?*

"Kyle!" Cora called out. She waited, but no one appeared in the exit. She called his name again, hoping the reason she hadn't seen him was because he'd already exited out the other side.

Darnell fell backward down the aisle. Kyle clung to the detached chairs as they slid from the plane's movement. He looked up to see Darnell get to his feet and head toward the incoming water, which had already risen to the height of the seats in the back.

Kyle stepped over the captain's body and watched the remaining passengers in line for the exits practically fall over each other to get to the openings.

"What are you doing?" Kyle called after the corporal.

"That guy's gonna drown!" he shouted without turning around.

Kyle waded down the aisle after him. The water had risen to his knees when he rushed past an unconscious man and an older woman still strapped into her seat next to him. In the dim light, Kyle recognized him as the man Cora had tried to help earlier, and he realized he wasn't unconscious, but dead.

He stopped and went back to their row.

"Do you need help getting off?" he asked the woman.

She shook her head. Kyle glanced at Darnell, who was nearly waist deep in water.

"I'm not getting off without my husband."

"It's too late for him. You need to get off *now*. We're the last ones on board." Kyle didn't wait for her response before starting after the corporal. "Darnell! Stop! He's done for."

Darnell slowed. Kyle reached for his arm.

"Hell, he might've even gotten out. But if not, you'll get yourself killed."

Darnell stared at the rear galley as water flowed up to Kyle's torso. He pulled on the corporal's arm. "Come on."

Darnell didn't move. For a moment, Kyle thought he was going to continue after the passenger into a deathtrap before Darnell turned to face him.

"Okay," he said.

Kyle turned, and they treaded up the aisle as fast as they could through the rising water. Kyle pushed a floating suitcase out of his way. He was dismayed to see the older woman hadn't moved from her seat.

"Ma'am, you have to get off!"

"*Now!*" Kyle added when he reached her row. Water was up to her knees.

The woman didn't move. Kyle wondered if she might be confused. It had grown too dark inside the plane to see her face clearly. He reached forward to help unbuckle her seatbelt.

She slapped his hand away. "I'm not leaving my husband." Her voice was steady, confident.

"The plane is *sinking*. I'm sorry, but we don't have time to get him out. If you don't come now, you'll die."

Despite the firmness in her voice, he again worried she didn't understand what was happening.

"It's my choice," she said. "And I'm choosing to stay with my hus—"

The plane groaned from beneath them before the tail dropped lower, causing Darnell and Kyle to fall back down the aisle, until they were swimming in neck-deep water. The tail sank farther beneath the surface as they fought against the rising water.

There was a sharp *hiss* as Darnell inflated his life vest. If he'd been wearing one, Kyle would've done the same, but he hadn't grabbed his from under his seat. His head went under and he swam forward. He'd never been a great swimmer, but he told himself this wasn't the time to dwell on it. Darnell grabbed him by the armpit and pulled him forward until he could get his footing on the aisle. Together, they treaded uphill toward the exits.

When they got close to the woman, she was nearly submerged in water. The plane creaked. It tilted to the side as the left emergency exit began to fill with water.

Darnell fell against the empty seats behind her. Kyle managed to keep his footing but struggled to reach the woman with his outstretched arms. He dove beneath the surface and searched for her seatbelt in the dark.

He felt himself float toward the surface and took a couple strokes to push himself down. His hand brushed an unmoving, floating arm, but there wasn't enough light to tell if it was the woman's or the man's. Darnell tugged on his arm.

Kyle allowed his head to surface. In the time he'd been underwater, the plane had shifted farther onto its side. The water level had nearly reached the luggage compartment over the couple's seats.

"You were right!" Darnell said, as Kyle took in a deep breath. "It's too late!"

Kyle reached again for the woman as Darnell put another hand on his arm and towed him in the direction of the emergency exit.

Darnell gripped him by the shoulders when he resisted. "It's the same deal as the guy in the back, man. We have to go!"

The plane turned beneath them with a violent pitch. Kyle looked back at the woman and her husband as the water rushing in through the exit covered them. There was nothing to do but follow the corporal toward the exit.

CHAPTER FORTY-TWO

From the evacuation slide still attached to the front exit, Alana watched in horror as the plane tipped on its side. Although it was sinking from back to front, water began to flow into the exit beside them. There was just enough light from the flashing beacon on the adjacent larger raft for her to make out the silhouette of the wing on the other side of the plane as it lifted into the air.

Alana and the older woman next to her had been able to let go of the raft beside them after someone threw its mooring line to a man behind her. Her eyes darted to the flooded exit.

"Don't we need to cut our ties?" she called to the flight attendant in the darkness.

Others in Alana's smaller raft started to panic. A wave came over the side of their slide, soaking Alana and those beside her. Alana leaned forward and grabbed onto the people next to her so she didn't topple over the edge. She struggled for something else to hold onto as the slide dipped to the side from the increasing swell.

"The ties should break on their own from the tension!" Linda's voice came from somewhere in the adjacent raft.

"But there's a small knife inside the flap at the top of the slide!"

The sides of the evacuation slide weren't as tall as those on the larger rafts. The wind had picked up since they landed, and Alana shivered beneath her drenched clothes. If the ocean swell picked up anymore, she worried they might not stay afloat until their rescue.

"It's too dark to find it! We could be dragged under!" a woman yelled.

"We can't see!" a man shouted. "We need your flashlight!"

The plane tilted in their direction as it continued to fill with water.

"Here!"

A hand reached through the darkness from the other raft toward Alana holding a knife and a flashlight. She grabbed them both and crawled through the crowded passengers toward the plane. She ran her hand along the inflated side connected to the plane until she felt a thin tie. Careful not to puncture the raft, she severed it before feeling for the second one. A deep metallic groan erupted from the aircraft before it dropped lower into the sea. Alana heard a snap, and the raft began drifting away from the sinking aircraft.

The movement caused Alana to lose her balance, and she fell against the side of the raft, dropping the knife into the water. Heart pounding, she sank below the slide's edge, clinging to the flashlight with shaking hands. Passengers around her gasped as the plane slowly disappeared from their view, but Alana didn't turn around. She would be glad to never see that plane again.

She put a hand on her belly, still in shock she'd survived the landing. She thought of Eddie. Was he contacted for a ransom? If so, how much did he pay for her life?

A few minutes later, the sky was completely dark, aside from a full moon. She realized they were lucky there was still daylight when the nurse made the water landing.

The somber faces around her were partially lit by the flashlight Alana still held in her hand. The bigger raft was still beside them. Two beacon lights shone from its side.

There were other rafts, but she wasn't sure how many. She turned and scanned the darkness until she spotted two sets of lights, just like the ones on the raft beside her. They were on either side of them, in opposite directions. She couldn't tell how far away they were, but one was definitely too far to swim.

She was about to ask if anyone knew how long until they'd be rescued when she saw lights flashing overhead. The plane's engine grew louder as the lights flew toward them. A small pink flare was shot off in the adjoining raft.

"That must be the Coast Guard," someone said.

There was a loud splash upwind of them just before the lights soared directly over their rafts. Alana remembered hearing something earlier about them coming to drop off supplies.

She'd also overheard that a cruise ship would be picking them up, but she prayed they wouldn't have to wait all night for it. Images of wooden lifeboats overfilled with survivors from the Titanic came to her mind. It seemed crazy after what they'd been through, but for some reason, being stranded in the middle of the dark ocean in nothing but a raft crammed with people seemed almost scarier than being on a hijacked flight.

"We're taking on water!" someone screamed.

Alana put her hand on the bottom of the slide. It was completely submerged. She thought she'd just been cold from getting soaked earlier. Alana tried to sit up, but the slide was at an angle, dipping into the ocean behind her.

She reached her hand behind her and felt the rush of a stream of water filling the back of the slide. The edge of the slide felt less firm than it had earlier. They were not only taking on water, but their slide was deflating.

"She must've cut the raft when she severed our ties!"

Alana recognized the slurred words of the drunk man who'd been seated behind her.

"I didn't cut the raft," she said. "I only cut one of the cords. The other one snapped as the plane sank."

"Maybe the cord tore a hole in the slide when it broke away," another male voice said in the darkness. "But it doesn't matter how. We need to fix it!"

Alana pointed the flashlight toward the bottom of their raft. "The water's rising." She was now sitting in a few inches of water.

"We have a patch kit!" a woman yelled from the adjacent raft. "But we need the flashlight to find it!"

Alana held the flashlight out as a man got to his knees and reached for it from the other side of the slide. As soon as the man had taken it, a large wave came over the side of the slide. Their sinking raft rolled as the wave moved beneath them, causing the man with the flashlight to lose his balance. Alana watched him fall against the edge. The beam of the flashlight shone toward the sky before it flew through the air and plopped into the water.

"Nooo!" the man shouted.

Alana covered her mouth with her hand. The cold water had risen almost to her waist. She pulled the toggle and inflated her life vest. Others around her did the same. She turned around as a rush of water came over the back of the slide.

"We're sinking!" she cried.

"Is there another flashlight?" someone yelled.

"No," Linda answered from the adjacent raft. "There's only one in each raft, and the slides don't have one."

A few people cried out beside Alana as water filled the back of the slide.

She pushed against the tightly crammed passengers. "We need to move forward!"

The other passengers slid over, giving them only inches of more space. "There's nowhere to go!"

"We need a patch kit!" a man said.

"It's too late!" Alana said. The sides of the raft on her end disappeared beneath the surface. She heard several hisses of air as the others on the slide inflated their life vests. The water was colder than she expected. She inhaled several short, sharp breaths as the water came up to her chest. Alana began treading water beneath her life vest with those around her as the bottom of the slide sank beneath them.

One by one, more water-activated lights blinked through the darkness until the raft completely sank, leaving more than a dozen of them bobbing in the dark water.

The lights moved toward the flashing beacon as Alana and the others swam toward the safety of the nearby raft.

"We're full—you can't come in!" a man hollered as they approached the raft.

Alana kept paddling through the cold water toward the raft. He couldn't be serious. They had to help them. *Right?*

"Let me in!" someone shouted from the water.

"Yes, let them in!" a woman said from the raft.

"No!" the man's voice was harsher now. "We've already taken on water from the swell. There's no way we can bring on over a dozen people. Unless we want to sink!"

"Please, help us!" a woman cried from the water. It sounded like the white-haired woman she'd held hands with during the landing.

Another voice responded from the raft. "We *can't*."

"Please!" Alana kept swimming toward the raft with the others.

There was arguing on the raft. Someone was pleading with the others to let a few of them on.

"No!"

"Didn't the Coast Guard drop off more rafts? Have them get in one of those!"

"They can't find them in the dark! And they could get hypothermia!"

"We'll *all* be in the water if we let them on! They could capsize us just trying to get in!"

The raft drifted away from them at a faster pace than they could swim. The waves were growing stronger. While Alana's life vest kept her afloat, it was hard to swim through the choppy sea. Her clothes dragged against the water as she moved.

There were pleas from the passengers around her as the raft moved farther away.

"Swim to the raft that was on the other side of the plane!" someone yelled across the water. "It had more room!"

Alana turned and saw the other raft's flashing beacon in the distance. The light from the moon reflected on the ocean's rippling surface between her and the raft. A wave came over the back of her head. She coughed and blinked the salt water out her eyes.

"Fine, let's go," someone shouted from the water.

Alana watched blinking lights from the others' life vests move in the direction of the other raft. Water sprayed her face as someone frantically thrashed their arms against the water as they swam past her. She turned away from the splashing, guessing it was the drunk man.

"Help us! We need a raft!" the man hollered as he swam toward the other raft.

Alana watched the flashing lights from the others swim farther away. She wasn't a strong swimmer. Her body shivered beneath the rolling waves. She could hear people still arguing in the raft behind her. She turned toward the voices. The raft was slowly drifting away from her, but it was still much closer than the others.

"Come on! You need to swim!"

The voice came from the water. It sounded like the older woman from first class. Alana turned, seeing a flashing light not too far ahead of her. She could still hear the splashes coming from the drunk man's panicked strokes. Alana swallowed her fears and swam toward the woman.

Alana watched some of the flashing lights reach the other raft as she swam in the woman's direction. Maybe the raft was closer than it looked. The sound of the drunk man's obnoxious splashing carried across the water. The light from his life vest was halfway between her and the raft, his chaotic movements not transferring to speed.

"Heellp!" he cried between splashes. "Heellpp meee! I need—" His voice morphed into a shrill scream. His scream turned to a gurgle then silence as the light from his life vest disappeared beneath the waves.

Alana froze in the now quiet waters.

His light reappeared on the surface and once again he thrashed against the waves. "Ahhh—"

There was another splash and then nothing.

"*What was that?*" someone shouted from the raft.

Hyperventilating, Alana searched the dark waters for a sign of the drunk man's light.

Aside from Alana and the woman ahead of her, there were only two other lights still in the water. And they had almost reached the raft.

"Pull us in!" one of them said. "Get us out of the water!"

"Come on!" the older woman called to her. "Let's move!"

But Alana remained frozen as the woman swam toward the raft. The woman had only made a few strokes when a cry erupted from the water. Her arms flailed atop the surface before she was pulled under. Alana swam backward as the light from the woman's life vest disappeared.

Alana felt something brush the bottom of her foot. Pulse pounding, she went still. Her eyes searched frantically beneath the surface. She was the only one left in the water.

Up ahead, the light from the woman's life vest bobbed to the surface. But there was no sound. No movement. Alana wanted to call out to her, but she was too terrified to speak. She held her breath as a dark figure erupted from the water and pulled the woman under a second time.

"Noo!" Alana felt through the water for the woman, but she was gone.

Alana covered her own flashing light with her hand. She forced herself to go still, trying not to attract the attention of the hungry beasts lurking below.

"Come on!" someone yelled from the raft in the distance.

There was no way she could reach the raft without being attacked like the other two. Slowly, she kicked her feet one by one to propel herself backward. Something grabbed her beneath her armpits.

She let out a scream as she was lifted out of the water.

"It's okay," a man said.

Alana felt the side of the inflated raft as she was pulled over the side. She landed on her back inside the raft, squeezed between several pairs of legs. Trembling, she sat up and looked back at the water, willing there to be a sign of life amidst the darkness. But there was nothing besides the waves lapping against the side of the raft.

She hunkered down between the bodies of those pressed tightly around her.

"What happened out there?" someone asked. "We heard screaming."

"There's sharks in the water."

A woman beside Alana gasped.

"*Sharks!*" someone shrieked.

"Take a headcount of how many you brought on!" Alana recognized Linda's voice as she called out to the other raft.

Someone pushed through the others beside her and draped a coat over her shoulders.

"Here, this will help warm you up."

Alana couldn't see the woman's face, but she sounded like the nurse who'd landed the plane.

"Do you have any injuries?"

"Um. No, I don't think so." Alana's teeth chattered between her words.

The nurse pulled the coat tighter around Alana's shoulders.

"We've brought ten people into our raft!" someone shouted from across the water.

"We're missing two passengers!" Linda yelled from the other side of the raft.

Alana tried to look for a sign of the two who'd been attacked, but the people who tightly surrounded her blocked her view of the water. She strained to hear any sounds coming from the surrounding waters. Nothing.

The passengers around her grew quiet as the raft bobbed atop the sea. She closed her eyes, and tears slid down her cheeks.

"I see lights!"

Alana opened her eyes. It was still dark. She wasn't sure how many hours had passed since she'd been pulled from the water. She immediately remembered the sight of the woman being attacked and dragged under by the shark.

"That must be the cruise ship!" the same voice said.

Alana sat up straighter and saw an abundance of lights coming toward them on the horizon. Linda sent off a large flare from their raft. Alana spotted a second flare from a different raft in the distance.

"Thank God!" exclaimed a woman beside her.

Alana's lip trembled as tears welled in her eyes. *Yes,* she thought. *Thank God indeed.*

CHAPTER FORTY-THREE

Cora stared over the cruise ship railing at the dark water moving beneath them, thinking of their plane resting on the bottom. Kyle leaned against the railing beside her, and she wondered if he was thinking the same thing. A cool breeze came over them.

When she'd first spotted him in the ship's dining hall, they'd run to each other's arms. It felt a little ridiculous given they'd just met, but she couldn't help it. She'd spent the entire time in the life raft wondering if he'd made it out alive before the plane sank.

The cruise ship was still searching for the other evacuation slide with the help of a Coast Guard helicopter. According to Linda, there were fourteen passengers in it. Unlike the rafts, the evacuation slides had no beacon lights or flares. It also wouldn't have fared as well against the open ocean, and the swell had picked up in the hours since they'd landed.

If only they'd let the passengers from the slide into their raft. Cora had tried to let them in, but the others wouldn't have it. Although maybe they *would've* capsized if they'd allowed them all into their raft. She'd never know. At least they'd pulled Alana Garcia in before she was attacked. She only wished they'd been able to save the two others.

Cora and Kyle looked up at the sound of the search helicopter as it soared over the cruise ship.

"Have they found them yet?"

Cora turned to see Darnell standing on the other side of Kyle.

"Not yet," Kyle said.

Her eyes followed the helicopter's spotlight as it canvased the dark choppy sea. "I hope it's not too late."

"Me too," the corporal said.

The helicopter hovered, and Cora spotted the bright yellow life vests that filled the gray slide. "It's them!"

The passengers were huddled together, and they waved their arms beneath the spotlight. The cruise ship slowed, and two orange rescue boats were lowered into the water from one of the decks below.

Cora's jaw dropped. "I really thought they were gone."

Kyle wrapped his arm around her. It looked like all fourteen passengers were still in the slide.

"They made it," he said.

The ship's engines idled, and Cora watched the two rescue crafts speed toward the evacuation slide. The passengers on the raft looked soaked. The three of them looked on in silence until the boats reached the remaining passengers.

Darnell took a step back from the railing. "On that note, I'm gonna go back inside and see if there's anything more I can do to help."

Kyle turned and extended his hand. "Thanks for all your help today. And for getting me off that plane before it was too late."

"You're welcome." He turned to Cora. "And that was one hell of a landing. I'll see you two inside."

Darnell left them alone on the deck, and Cora sank against the detective in relief. "I'm so glad they found them." Even though she knew it was out of her hands, part of her still felt responsible for them after landing the plane.

"So am I. They were out there on their own for a long time."

The two boats idled beside the raft. One by one, the passengers were helped into the boats. A spotlight from the cruise ship replaced the helicopter's bright beam after all the passengers were safely inside the rescue boats. The helicopter retreated to the ship's landing pad.

"I wonder if I could cruise back to Seattle," Cora said. "I'm not sure if I can get back on a plane anytime soon." But she knew she'd have to. And after the day's events, she wanted nothing more than to hold her children.

"I'm only getting on one if you're on it." He'd been given a change of dry clothes by one of the stewards as they prepared staterooms for the survivors. He was indistinguishable from a tourist in his khaki shorts and Tommy Bahama shirt. He grinned. "*And* if we're in First Class. Even with the emergency landing, that was still way better than how I usually fly in economy."

Cora raised her eyebrows at his attempt at humor.

"I shouldn't joke when there were people who lost their lives today," he said. "I guess I'm used to using humor to cope with my work. The truth is, we're really lucky to be standing here." He smiled. "Good thing you turned out to be such a good pilot."

Cora smiled back as she shook her head. She leaned against him, pressing her head against his chest as Kyle wrapped his arm around her shoulders.

He leaned his head toward hers. "You know, for a moment in the cockpit I thought you were going to kiss me."

Cora smiled and turned to face him. "You must've been a little delusional from your injuries."

He laughed. Their faces were only inches apart.

"I don't think so." He gently brushed a strand of hair back from her face. His expression turned serious. "I don't think I've ever met anyone as remarkable as you. Umm...."

His voice faltered for the first time that day.

He cleared his throat. "I was wondering...."

Cora contained a smile. *Was he nervous? Now?*

"I meant it when I asked about going to dinner with you when we were in the cockpit. Would you like to go on a date when we get back to Seattle?"

His words were nearly drowned out by the *whir* of rotor blades as the chopper descended onto the ship. Since the ship wouldn't reach the Big Island until morning, the helicopter crew was planning to take a few passengers with suspected concussions and broken bones back to the nearest hospital.

When the announcement had been made about the helicopter making a run to the hospital, she had tried to get Kyle to go since he'd lost consciousness after Mila's attack and then hit his head during the landing. But he'd refused. She suspected he'd downplayed his injuries to allow others to go in his place. And since he wasn't displaying any residual symptoms other than the bump on his forehead, she hadn't argued. At any rate, Cora was glad that she was being relieved of her duties as a nurse now that emergency medical aid was on board.

Cora leaned into Kyle's ear so he could hear her above the rhythmic chop of the helicopter. "Yes."

He turned to her with wide eyes. "Yes?"

She bit her lip. "Yes."

He leaned forward, bringing his face closer. "I knew you wanted to kiss me earlier."

Cora grinned. "And how would you know that?"

"I'm a detective, remember?"

He brought his lips to hers before she could respond.

CHAPTER FORTY-FOUR

Early the next morning, a guard led Asha down a sterile hallway at the SeaTac Federal Detention Center. Last night, she'd been allowed to call Aaden before being taken to her cell. He was furious, having spoken to Rosalyn after hearing of Asha's confession on the news.

His words still stung. *Why didn't you tell me?* he'd asked. *We could've gone to the police. Instead, you helped those terrorists kill people. And ruined our family.* She feared he might never speak to her again. Asha had lain awake all night listening to the sounds of other prisoners until she finally cried herself to sleep just before dawn.

The guard stopped and used her ID badge to unlock a door with a small window in the middle. There was a loud beep followed by a click as the door unlocked. The guard opened the door and escorted Asha inside. Asha stepped into the small meeting room and saw that her young court-appointed attorney was already waiting for her.

"Good morning," her attorney said as the guard secured Asha's cuffs to the table.

This was apparently a normal day for her attorney. But there was nothing normal about it for Asha. It felt like hell on earth.

"Good morning." Asha looked down at her bright orange jumpsuit.

"I have some good news," her attorney said.

She looked across the table at him.

"Your family in Somalia has been rescued."

Asha brought her hand to her mouth, but it was caught short by the handcuff. She tried to speak, but no words came.

"The US deployed a group of Navy SEALS from Camp Lemonnier in Djibouti to your home village in Somalia. I was informed this morning that they were able to rescue all your remaining relatives who were being held hostage at their village. The Al-Shabaab terrorists were killed except for one, who is in US custody."

Asha choked back her tears. "What about Flight 385?"

"You didn't hear?" He looked surprised. "I thought the feds would've told you last night."

She shook her head.

"The plane landed on the ocean. Safely. It sank quickly, but most of the passengers made it to safety. Aside from the three known hijackers on board, there were nine casualties."

Nine people died because of what she did. She'd known last night there had been casualties, just not how many. A wave of relief came over her. While those nine deaths would forever haunt her, it could've been so much worse.

"Now," her attorney said, as he folded his hands atop the table between them. "I need to talk to you about the charges you're facing. They are very serious, as I know you're aware. Since deaths occurred as a result of your aiding and abetting the terrorists who hijacked Flight 385, you are looking at twenty years to life in prison."

Her relief over her family's safety quickly turned to despair of leaving her two daughters without a mother. She knew she was looking at serious time in prison, but not life. Hearing him say the words felt like she'd had the wind knocked out of her.

"But, for your cooperation, and, if you plead guilty to all charges, the prosecutor's office is willing to consider a plea bargain. That means that you would avoid a trial and receive a more lenient sentence." He paused to let the words sink in.

"How lenient?" Asha asked.

"I'm going to meet with the prosecutor after this, so I'll have an answer for you later today. But I'm hoping to get it reduced to less than twenty, possibly even under fifteen. *If* they agree to that, I advise you should take it.

"But I'll find out exactly what they're offering before you accept," he added.

"Okay," she said after a moment. She *was* guilty, so pleading that way didn't seem like a large price to pay in exchange for a shorter imprisonment.

"Good." The young attorney nodded. He stood from his seat, signaling their meeting was over. "Let's hope the prosecutor comes back with a reasonable offer, because I think it's your best option."

He turned around when he reached the door. Through the small window, Asha could see the guard waiting on the other side.

"And I'm glad the rest of your family is okay."

Tears spilled down her cheeks as he left the room and the guard reentered. Without a word, the guard detached her cuffs from the table and led her into the hallway. While being escorted back to her cell, Asha thought back on the events of the last two days.

When they reached her cell door, she thought about what her attorney had said. His words filled her with an overwhelming sense of both relief and sadness. It was a great consolation that her remaining family in Somalia was alive.

If only she'd gone to the police right away instead of helping those terrorists hijack Flight 385.

CHAPTER FORTY-FIVE

"I'm so glad you're okay, baby."

Alana smiled at the sound of Eddie's soothing voice. She was perched on the end of the bed in the interior cabin the cruise line had given her for the night. The ship was just coming into port, and she'd called Eddie the moment she had service.

"I've never been so scared in my life." She picked up the last piece of fruit from her room service tray on the bed beside her.

"Me neither," Eddie said. "I got the best and worst news of my life yesterday. Finding out you're pregnant, and then that I might lose you. My assistant told me the news of the hijacking during last night's meeting. It was terrifying."

"But I was one of the lucky ones." Her stomach turned as she thought of the two passengers who'd been taken by sharks. She felt a stab of guilt as she set down her fork. "I couldn't help but wonder if I was the reason behind the attack. For money. Were you contacted for a ransom or anything?"

"No. Not a ransom. The FBI sent a couple agents to my house when they learned of the connection between me and one of the flight attendants. And, of course, you being on the flight."

"A connection?" She thought of Mila, the bitchy first-class attendant who was part of the hijacking. But how would Eddie know her?

"Yes." His voice was calm. *Almost too calm,* Alana thought. "Turns out she worked for me as a pilot on the Gulfstream. I ended up having to fire her about two years ago. She was found to have cocaine in her possession not long after, while she was flying a corporate jet for someone else."

Alana vaguely recalled hearing about it in the news. It was before she'd met Eddie, and she hadn't paid much attention.

"So, it was about you? But if not money, then what? Does the FBI know who the other hijackers were? Did you know them?"

"As far as I'm aware, they don't know yet."

Alana's mind was reeling. If the hijacking was about Eddie, then why didn't they contact him for money? It seemed unfathomable that Mila would have been willing to kill a plane full of people, including herself, to get revenge on Eddie for firing her.

There was a knock on her door. "Hang on. There's someone at my door."

Alana slid off the crisp white duvet and walked the two strides to her cabin door. She squinted through the peephole. She wasn't ready to talk to any reporters. Two men in suits stood outside her room. One of them held up a government ID.

Alana cracked open her door, keeping her phone against her ear.

"Alana Garcia?" one of them asked.

"Yes?"

"I'm Agent Kahele, and this is Agent Matsuo. I'm with the FBI, and he's with the Honolulu Office of Homeland Security. We're assisting in the investigation of the hijacking and we'd like to ask you a few questions."

"How did you—I mean, we haven't even docked yet."

"We took a helicopter once the ship was in range," Kahele said. "May we come in?"

"Sure." She put her finger in the air. "Just one second." She turned her head away from the agents and spoke into her phone. "Sorry, Eddie, I have to go. Some agents want to speak to me about the hijacking."

"Okay.... Call me back as soon as you're done. And don't tell them any more than you need to. Love you."

"Love you too." She dropped her phone to her side. *Any more than I need to?* She turned back to the men standing in her doorway. She opened the door wider. "Come on in."

Agent Matsuo nodded. "Thank you."

She stepped aside to give them room to enter.

"Please, have a seat." She motioned toward a small couch against the wall.

The agents sat down beside each other on the couch, and Alana sat across from them in the only chair in the room.

"First of all, we're sorry for what has probably been a very traumatic day," Agent Kahele started.

Alana crossed her legs. "Thank you."

"How long have you been in a relationship with Eddie Clarke?"

"A little over six months."

"Are you aware that Mila Morina, the flight attendant who tried to take over the plane, had worked for Eddie as his private pilot?"

Alana shook her head. "No. Well, not until just now." She looked between the two agents, whose facial expressions were hard to read. "Eddie told me he fired her two years ago. Then, she was found in possession of cocaine."

Agent Kahele leaned forward. "Did Mila Morina say anything to you that would indicate you were being targeted during the hijacking?"

"No."

"What about the two male hijackers? Did they ever approach you? Or say anything to you?"

"No. Nothing. But you think Eddie, and I, were the reason they hijacked the plane?"

The agents exchanged a look. Matsuo answered. "It's still very early in the investigation. But yes, we believe Eddie, and yourself, were the targets. Eddie was sent a photo of you on the plane less than three hours into the flight with a strict set of demands if he wanted you to live."

Alana felt her jaw drop open. "I just talked to Eddie. He said he didn't receive a ransom request."

"The demands weren't for money. He was told to post a video on all his social media accounts confessing to various wrongdoings, including fraud and sexual assault. And to announce that he was stepping down from his largest company."

Alana hadn't bothered to check social media before calling Eddie. But she wondered how much damage had been done to his reputation, and his companies, after posting something like that. He'd be devastated if he lost Clarke Pharmaceuticals; it was his whole life aside from her.

"So, Mila and these two men were going to take down a plane of innocent people out of some sort of revenge?"

Agent Kahele spoke this time. "It appears that way."

"Do you know who the two men were?"

"Not yet. We were hoping to be able to ID their bodies, but we'll have to wait and see if they can be recovered from the crash site."

Kahele added, "That's all our questions for now, unless you have anything to add?"

"Not that I can think of."

The agent pressed his palms to his knees and stood from the couch. He held out his business card to Alana. "Thanks for your time. If you think of anything else, please give us a call."

Alana accepted the card and looked absently at the address and email on it. "I will."

Agent Matsuo pointed toward the worn-out copy of *The Count of Monte Cristo* laying atop the coffee table as the agents moved toward the door. Its damp pages were ruffled from its time in the water. "That's a great book. Did you manage to keep that from the flight?"

Alana followed his gaze. She felt a twinge of guilt for having it, knowing they weren't supposed to take any belongings off the plane. But if it weren't for the cop, they could've all been dead. It seemed the least she could do.

And no one noticed when she slipped it into her front sweatshirt pocket before getting off.

"Oh, it's not mine. But yes, I rescued it from the flight. I meant to give it back to the man sitting across from me, but we ended up in different rafts. I heard him say he'd been reading it for years."

"Yeah, it's a long one. But it's worth the read. Best revenge story ever."

Alana recalled the cop on the plane saying the exact same thing to the woman sitting next to him. But she couldn't stop thinking about the video Eddie had posted.

"I'm sorry," Alana said as Kahele reached for the door. "But is Eddie in any sort of legal trouble after posting that video? I mean, could he be arrested for admitting to those things? And what about his company?" Maybe that was why he didn't tell her on the phone. He didn't want her to worry about how much he'd lost in order to save her.

The agents exchanged an awkward glance before Kahele answered. "He didn't post it, ma'am."

Alana moved her gaze to Agent Matsuo. "I—I don't understand."

"He didn't concede to the hijackers' demands," Matsuo said.

Alana looked back at Kahele. Maybe Eddie hadn't seen the message in time. Three hours into her flight would have been close to when his meeting started.

"They sent him a text message, you said?"

"And a phone call. When Eddie answered, it was a computerized voice demanding that he comply with their demands if…" Agent Matsuo paused. "If he wanted you to live."

When Eddie answered. She felt like she'd been punched in the gut. *Had Eddie received these threats and then carried on with his big meeting as if nothing had happened?*

"Did he go to the police?" she asked.

"The FBI came to him." Matsuo exchanged a look with his counterpart. "Later that night," he added.

"Thanks for your time," Kahele said. "And you're free to go when the ship docks." He opened the door and stepped into the hall.

Matsuo brushed past her and followed Kahele out of her room, leaving Alana alone in the cabin.

She looked at her phone in her hand. *He didn't concede to the hijackers' demands.* Was Eddie's ego more important to him than her and their unborn child's lives? Did he think she wouldn't find out that he didn't take the necessary steps to save her?

She sank back into the uncomfortable chair across from the now empty couch. She tossed her phone onto the coffee table and brought her hands to her temples, staring at the tattered classic novel beside her phone. A male voice came over the Intercom in the hallway, startling her from her thoughts. Although the speaker was outside her room, the man's voice resounded through her cabin walls loud and clear.

"Good morning, passengers. This is your cruise director. We will be docking in less than thirty minutes. Once we have approval from the port authorities, I will make an announcement that you are free to disembark. Survivors of Flight 385, please return to your staterooms and wait to be interviewed by the agents who have come aboard our ship. Please do not attempt to disembark until you have been cleared by the investigating authorities. On behalf of *Hawaiian Cruise Line*, and all staff on board, we are honored to be part of the rescue mission to help you return home to your loved ones. Thank you."

Alana gathered the few belongings she still possessed and a few toiletries from the cabin bathroom to help her make the trip back to Seattle. How could she have been so blind? Eddie couldn't post a stupid video to save her, along with a plane full of other people?

No wonder he didn't tell her. *What a sociopathic prick.* Her hand fell protectively to her belly. Would he have even cared if she'd died? Apparently, it wouldn't be as bad as jeopardizing his fortune.

Mila thought she'd enact revenge by threatening what mattered most to Eddie. But she'd been wrong. He'd chosen his own success over Alana and their child.

Alana leaned forward and lifted the hefty leather-bound book from the table. She placed in on her lap and ran her thumb over its faded cover. Leaving him wouldn't be enough. He'd get over it.

If he couldn't take a simple action to save nearly two hundred lives, he wasn't the man she thought he was. It struck her that maybe Mila knew Eddie better than she did. But even Mila underestimated Eddie's profound selfishness.

Alana wouldn't make the same mistake.

If he cared more about his self-made empire than human lives, she'd be doing him a favor by taking it away from him. Stripping him of his company might be the only chance for him to find an ounce of decency within himself.

She'd seen Eddie log into his laptop countless times. And aside from him, no one would have access to it like she would: sleeping under his roof, unsuspected. It would be easy enough to use his fingerprint to unlock his phone if she slipped him a couple of the sleeping pills she'd been prescribed for insomnia.

Surely, there were plenty of competitive companies that would love to receive all the data she could access. China might be a good start. And if that wasn't enough, it wouldn't be that hard to plant some incriminating evidence on his computer.

Alana jumped when her phone vibrated atop the coffee table. She picked it up and saw it was Eddie calling.

"Hey baby."

"Hey. I hope I'm not interrupting. Are the agents still speaking with you?"

"No, they're gone. Just pretty standard stuff. They wanted to know if the hijackers said anything to me on the flight."

"Oh. Did they?"

"Nothing out of the ordinary."

"Did the agents say anything else?"

Like that you chose to save your own ass rather than save all our lives? "No, that was pretty much it."

"I'm so sorry for all you went through."

She could hear the relief in his voice. Relief that his cowardice hadn't been found out.

"I should call my sister. She's probably worried sick, and we're about to dock."

"Okay. I love you."

You don't love anyone but yourself. "I love you too."

"Call me again when you can."

"Before I go—remember you offered to let me use your private jet for the trip?"

"Yes."

"I think I'll take you up on it. For the way home. If that's okay?"

"Of course, baby. Just let me know when you want it."

"I will. Thanks." She tucked the thick novel under her arm as she ended the call and headed for the door.

CHAPTER FORTY-SIX

Whitney looked beyond the journalists who filled the blue padded chairs in the James S. Brady Press Briefing Room in the West Wing of the White House. She fixed her gaze on the camera crew at the back of the small theater and forced a smile.

"Good evening everyone."

The president had sent Whitney home for a few hours of sleep after they received the news of Flight 385's mostly-successful water landing. Although Whitney had returned to the White House first thing that morning, the administration instructed her to hold off on the press briefing until this evening so they could gather more information.

"As you are already aware, last night a passenger on Pacific Air 385 made an intact water landing on the Pacific Ocean after the flight was hijacked on its way from Seattle to Honolulu. In addition to the three hijackers, there were nine casualties including both pilots. One of the deceased hijackers has been identified as Mila Morina, who was a flight attendant on Flight 385. The identities of the other two hijackers are still unknown, as they boarded the plane using stolen IDs. The FBI is hoping to have more information once they have recovered their bodies from the crash site.

"The Department of Homeland Security and FBI are working together to investigate the motivation behind the hijacking. The terrorist organization Al-Shabaab was quick to claim responsibility for the attack. However, the extent of their involvement is still being investigated."

Whitney glanced at her notes on top of the wood podium.

"We can confirm that one of the guns was planted on the flight by an airline cleaner who had been sent a video from Somali terrorists showing the execution of her uncle. The video threatened the lives of her entire extended family if she didn't comply. Early this morning, Navy SEALs were deployed from Camp Lemonnier and completed a successful rescue mission of all the Somali citizens who were held hostage by Al-Shabaab.

"The second gun is believed to have been brought onto the flight by Mila Morina, the flight attendant who bypassed airport security. Policy changes to this process are already being addressed."

Whitney heard murmuring among the reporters as she slid the top page of her notes to the side of the large podium before continuing.

"Mila Morina had previously been employed by and filed a lawsuit against Clarke Pharmaceuticals founder Eddie Clarke, whose girlfriend was on board Flight 385. Eddie Clarke was also contacted by the hijackers during the flight via a satellite device. Currently, investigators are considering that the motives of this hijacking were not terror, but personal revenge, possibly a ransom."

Whitney looked up at the packed room of journalists' familiar faces. "There are still many unanswered questions, but I can assure you that the Department of Homeland Security, including the TSA, as well as the FBI are conducting a thorough investigation. And, with that, I'll take questions."

Nearly every hand in the room shot up. Whitney steeled herself for the barrage of questions and accusations that would follow.

She pointed at a woman in the front row. "Erin, go ahead."

CHAPTER FORTY-SEVEN

Cora checked her reflection another time in the full-length mirror of her master bedroom. She hadn't been on a first date in so long, she'd had no idea what to wear. Her doorbell rang. She smoothed her sleeveless blouse and took one last glance at her fitted jeans before turning from the mirror.

She moved down the stairs of her Briarcliff home as quick as her heels would allow. Her mother had taken the kids for the night, and the house felt strangely quiet. When she reached the entryway, she could see Kyle's muscular frame outside the frosted glass of her front door.

Her heart felt like it skipped a beat. She hadn't seen him since they got off the cruise ship in Hawaii three weeks ago. She ran her hand over her hair before opening the door.

The detective flashed her a nervous smile. Cora was glad she wasn't the only one with the jitters. She wasn't sure what the rules of dating were anymore, but she'd found it endearing when he'd offered to pick her up.

"Hi," he said, holding out a large bouquet of tropical flowers. "It's nice to see you again."

"Thank you." Cora accepted the flowers. "You too." Seeing him brought back a flood of emotions from their horrific flight as well as her instant attraction to him.

"Do you want to come in for a sec? I'll just put these in water."

"Sure." He closed the door behind him and followed her toward the back of the house.

Cora led him into the kitchen, where she grabbed a vase from one of the cupboards and filled it with some water from the sink. "I love Bird of Paradise. It's one of my favorite flowers."

"I'm glad you like them." He leaned back against her kitchen island. "How are your kids? Do they know about anything that happened on our flight—and what a hero their mother is?"

She shook her head. "Not really. They're so young, and I didn't want to worry them after what happened to their father. But I'll tell them when they're older." She smiled. "And they're doing good, thanks. My mom is watching them tonight."

Their eyes met when she looked up after putting the tropical flowers into the vase. It seemed strange that she'd only met him a few weeks ago. After all they'd been through, it felt like she'd known him much longer.

"I saw on the news that they recovered some bodies from the plane."

Kyle nodded. "Yeah, six bodies were found still inside the plane on the ocean floor. The copilot's body is still missing, along with the two hijackers."

"And the FBI still doesn't know who they were?"

"No. And if they don't recover their bodies, it's possible they never will."

Their arms brushed as he walked beside her out of the kitchen.

"You look beautiful," he added.

Cora smiled self-consciously. "So do you. I mean, you look good too."

Kyle brought his hand up playfully to his short-cropped hair. "Well, thank you. I *did* spend a few hours on my hair."

They shared a laugh before he opened the front door for Cora.

"Actually," he said when they stepped onto her front porch, "I was a little nervous to see you again. I haven't been on a proper date in a long time."

"Me neither."

Their hands found each other's as they walked down her driveway.

"I haven't been able to stop thinking about you since that flight," he said when they reached his car.

She let go of his hand and moved to the passenger side of his car. Cora lifted her eyes to the drone of a commercial jet that flew overhead. Kyle followed her gaze.

"I've been thinking about you a lot, too." She tore her eyes from the plane and smiled. "And I think you still owe me for passing out there in the end."

He let out a short laugh. "You did perfectly fine without me. And I plan on making up for it tonight." He shot her a playful look over the roof of his car. "Since you said I could pick where we go for dinner."

She eyed him curiously.

"I made reservations at the Space Needle," he added. "I know it's more of a tourist spot. But I've lived in Seattle my whole life and never been up there. I thought we could take in the view without having to worry about how we'll get down."

EPILOGUE

Seven Months Later

The sound of two inmates' obnoxious laughter filled the recreational day-use room when Asha entered through the doorway. She kept her eyes down before taking a seat in one of the uncomfortable plastic chairs at an empty table, having learned the hard way that other inmates didn't like being stared at.

The day after the hijacking, a prominent criminal defense attorney had offered to defend her pro bono. After she declined the services of her court-appointed attorney, she'd taken her new lawyer's advice and rejected the federal prosecutor's plea deal. Instead, she'd pled not guilty and taken her chances in court.

Her trial ended yesterday, and the jury had been deliberating for over twenty-four hours. Asha had a sinking feeling that she'd made a mistake. Going to trial was a gamble, with only two extreme outcomes. If she was found guilty, she could get life in prison. Her attorney was confident they would win, but as the hours wore on, Asha's doubts grew.

She avoided eye contact with the other women and looked up at the small TV mounted to the upper corner of the room.

"How you doin' tonight, sweetheart?" an older inmate asked.

Asha met her gaze with caution. "Fine, thanks. How are you?"

The older woman nodded. "Oh, same old. You know. Your jury still deliberating?"

Asha nodded.

"That's not good. A long deliberation means a guilty verdict. Trust me, I know."

Asha blinked back tears, and both women turned their attention toward the TV as a familiar Seattle news reporter filled the screen. The reporter looked to be standing in front of a downtown skyscraper. The wind blew her long dark hair to the side as she spoke.

"Breaking news this evening in Seattle as we learn that Clarke Pharmaceuticals has been a victim of what some are calling the largest cybersecurity breach of the decade. Our sources have confirmed that personal information from all Clarke Pharmaceuticals employees, consumers, *and* clinical research trial participants has been compromised. We have also learned that the pharmaceutical tycoon's research data and pharmacological formulas have also been breached. An investigation is currently underway to find the culprits of this data breach, but sources are already speculating that a Chinese competitor is to blame."

An inmate let out a loud whistle from the table behind Asha.

"Are we bothering you?" another voice came from the table at the back of the room. Assuming they were speaking to someone else, Asha ignored the question.

The reporter continued. "While we're still learning the details of this massive cybersecurity incident, investigators believe that the breach occurred using the login credentials of the company's founder Eddie Clarke. This news comes fewer than seven months after Eddie Clarke's girlfriend, Alana Garcia, was a passenger on hijacked Flight 385. We'll have more updates on this later tonight."

A fist slammed against the table in front of Asha, making her jump. She looked up, recognizing the larger of the two inmates she'd passed on her way into the room. The woman brought her face within inches of Asha's. Asha shrank against her plastic seat.

"I *said*, Are. We. Bothering. You?"

Asha guessed the inmate weighed more than double what she did. Her breath was rancid, but Asha didn't turn away. She knew that even the slightest offense could provoke a fight. And this woman already looked provoked.

Asha shook her head. "No. You aren't bothering me."

The woman's cracked lips turned into a scowl. Her eyes narrowed. Asha's widened. The inmate pushed her palms against Asha's chest, sending her to the concrete floor. Her plastic chair fell on top of her, but the woman was quick to toss it aside.

"Guard!" Asha heard the older woman shriek from the corner of the room.

The angry woman raised her fist in the air. Asha brought her hands up protectively to her face with her arms in front of her chest. Asha closed her eyes before the impact from the first blow to her ribs.

"Stop!" Asha heard someone yell.

Her attacker got in another punch before two guards managed to pry her away from Asha.

"You're going back to the hole," she heard one of the guards say as they cuffed her attacker.

"Good." The large woman spit in Asha's direction before the guards hauled her out of the room. "I can't wait to get away from that terrorist *bitch*."

Asha pulled herself up using the support of her chair. The woman's words didn't rile her. She was used to it. What she'd done was no secret among the prisoners, and it hadn't helped her popularity.

"Asha Farar!" a guard barked from the doorway.

Asha turned, wondering if she'd be going to the hole too. The guards never seemed to care who started the fight.

"Your verdict's in. Let's go." The guard's voice was impatient as she withdrew a pair of handcuffs.

Ignoring the burn in her side, Asha moved toward the guard.

Asha sat beside her attorney and watched the jurors file into the jury box in the King County Federal District courtroom.

Asha stared at the jurors, trying to read their faces. They looked tired, but they kept their expressions neutral as they avoided eye contact with her. The inmate's words reverberated in Asha's mind. *A long deliberation means a guilty verdict.*

The judge instructed Asha and her attorney to stand and face the jury.

Asha stood and smoothed the front of the tailored suit her attorney had helped her buy for the trial. Aaden was seated on a bench behind them. She was thankful for his presence, even though she was still ashamed for all she'd put her husband through. She shot a nervous glance at her attorney, who momentarily placed a steady hand on Asha's shaking shoulders.

The presiding juror stood from his seat and cleared his throat. "The U.S. District Court for the Western District of Washington in the matter of the people of the United States versus Asha Absame Farar, case number…"

Asha closed her eyes and willed herself to listen over her pounding heart. The thought of never seeing her daughters outside of an occasional prison visit was unbearable.

"…find the defendant, Asha Absame Farar, not guilty in the crime of providing material support for terrorism."

Asha heard a cry escape from her lips as the juror continued.

"We find the defendant not guilty in the crime of conspiracy. We find the defendant not guilty in the crime of aiding and abetting terrorists. We find the defendant guilty in the crime of carrying a concealed firearm without a permit. And we find the defendant guilty in the crime of carrying a firearm into a restricted area."

Asha felt her knees start to buckle as the judge addressed the court. She pressed her hands atop the wood table for support.

"Asha Farar, in consideration of the offenses for which you now stand convicted, you are sentenced by order of the court to ninety days imprisonment in a house of correction and a $1,000 fine. The court will credit your time spent in confinement starting on the date of your arrest, and you are hereby released. Court is adjourned. Ms. Farar, you are free to go."

Asha's attorney wrapped her in an embrace. Held up by her lawyer, Asha reached her arm over the rail behind them. She felt Aaden's hand squeeze hers.

"Congratulations," her attorney spoke into her ear. "You're going home."

Alana placed a hand on her protruding belly and admired the newly decorated white and pink nursery. A smile came to her lips at the thought of meeting her baby daughter in less than a week. She felt a kick against her abdomen as she moved toward the large window overlooking the Pacific. She pushed the striped curtain aside and stared out at the ocean.

She'd purchased the Northern California beach house a few months ago with her own money, leading Eddie to believe they'd use it for family vacations. The authorities had yet to suspect her involvement in Clarke Pharmaceutical's colossal data breach. Maybe they would have if she'd accepted the payment offered by the Chinese pharmaceutical company that she had leaked all of Eddie's data to. But she had left no paper trail. Watching Eddie's reaction to his company's stocks plummet and the resulting scandal was payment enough.

Hundreds of lawsuits had already been filed against his company. Even if only a fraction of them won, Clark Pharmaceuticals would likely declare bankruptcy.

In the days following the cybersecurity breach, three women had come forward and publicly accused Eddie of sexual assault. Two of them had already filed civil lawsuits against Eddie, and Alana read a news article that morning that hinted there would be forthcoming criminal charges. The scandal had given Alana the perfect excuse to leave him without being implicated in his company's downfall.

An image flashed in her mind of Eddie tearfully pleading with her to stay when she left his home for the last time. She turned from the window and sat down in the pale pink rocking chair. Eddie was no longer her concern.

She was starting fresh. After what happened on Flight 385, she wasn't going to take the rest of her years for granted. She'd been given the gift of becoming a mother and planned on enjoying the best years of her life.

Kyle and Cora followed behind the White House Chief of Staff down the hallway toward the Oval Office.

The Chief of Staff nodded at a blonde woman walking in their direction. "Hey, Whit."

Kyle recognized the press secretary when she moved past him.

"Hi, Thomas," she replied without slowing her pace.

The hallway came to a corner, and Thomas stopped to open a door. "Right this way." He motioned for Kyle and Cora to step inside.

Kyle followed behind Cora and took in the grandeur of the Oval Office. He'd only ever seen it in pictures. Thomas directed them toward the pale-yellow flowered sofas in the middle of the room.

"Please, have a seat. The president will be with you shortly."

"Thank you," Cora said.

Kyle stepped atop the navy circular rug and took a seat next to her. The Chief of Staff retreated out the door they'd come in as a man in a dark suit entered the office. Without a word, the secret service member stood to the side of the doorway, staring straight ahead with a blank expression.

Cora smoothed her black dress atop her thighs and leaned into Kyle. "Are you nervous?"

"Yes." *But not to meet the president.* He could feel the small square jewelry box in his inside suit pocket. He planned to propose on their flight home. It seemed fitting given the way they had met. He only hoped she would find it as romantic as he did.

He eyed the elegant woman beside him and started to worry that he should have thought of something better. More impressive. He only had one shot to propose.

He placed his hand on her knee. "What about you?"

"A little. It's such a big deal. I can hardly believe we're sitting here."

"You deserve to be honored by the President. You're a hero, remember?"

She let out a deep breath. "I think I'm more nervous to meet her than I am to be on national TV. I just wish we didn't have to get back on a plane tonight. I don't know if I'll ever be able to fly again without feeling anxious."

"I have a really good feeling about our flight home."
Her eyes searched his.

"Plus," he added. "What are the odds of being on a hijacked flight *twice?*"

The door to the Oval Office opened. Kyle took her hand in his as they stood to their feet.

NOTE FROM THE AUTHOR

I had a great time writing this book with the help of my dad, a retired Air Force and airline pilot.

The initial idea for this story came to me a few years back, after the tragic disappearance of Malaysia Airlines Flight 370. That plane's disappearance highlighted the vulnerability we face as a passenger. It is one of the countless situations we encounter when our safety is beyond our control.

Creating the characters for this story forced me to imagine how people might act when faced with a life-or-death situation and whether it would bring out the best or the worst in them. Alana, in particular, grew on me toward the end.

I hope you enjoyed the ride as much as I did and that you are never on board a flight as eventful as Pacific Air Flight 385.

ACKNOWLEDGMENTS

I have to start by thanking my husband, Brett, for relentlessly supporting my writing.

Dad, thank you for your endless expertise in helping me write this book. This book would not have been the same without the wealth of knowledge you shared with me. Mom, thank you for your support and advice. And for introducing me to my first crime fiction novels and detective noir films.

Huge thanks to my editor, Bryan Tomasovich, for your insight and hard work. Your guidance over all my books has made me a better writer.

To Penny Lane, thanks for being more than a proofreader and for your invaluable help in fine-tuning my stories.

Special thanks to Detective Rolf Norton for taking the time to answer my questions and for the vitally important work you do to help our community.

Kylie, thank you for sharing your knowledge as a flight attendant with me and for being an avid reader of all my books.

Jenifer Ruff, Dan Alatorre, and Tim and Julie Browne, thanks so much for your encouragement and writing advice. Having author friends makes writing a book much more fun.

WANT MORE?

Get your FREE bonus content and new release
updates including a bonus chapter and
alternate epilogue to THE PILOT'S DAUGHTER
at AUDREYJCOLE.COM/sign-up

COMING 2022

PRE-ORDER NOW

EMERALD CITY THRILLERS

BY AUDREY J. COLE

THE RECIPIENT
INSPIRED BY MURDER
THE SUMMER NANNY
VIABLE HOSTAGE
FATAL DECEPTION

EMERALD CITY THRILLERS
BOOKS 1-5 BOXSET

ABOUT THE AUTHOR

Audrey J. Cole is a *USA TODAY* bestselling thriller author. She resides in the Pacific Northwest with her husband and two children. Before writing full time, she worked as a neonatal intensive care nurse for eleven years. She's also a pilot's daughter.

Connect with Audrey:

f facebook.com/AudreyJCole

BB bookbub.com/authors/Audrey-J-Cole

instagram.com/AudreyJCole/

You can also visit her website:
www.AUDREYJCOLE.com

CPSIA information can be obtained
at www.ICGtesting.com
Printed in the USA
LVHW030443220821
695831LV00002B/153